Sunsets

on the

Mountain

By

Susan M. Young

Dedication

For Mom.

An avid reader, my biggest fan, and the BEST MOM anyone could wish for.

Thank you for filling our home with stories, for always believing in mine, and for showing me what quiet strength and endless love look like.

This book is for you because every chapter I've ever written began with you in my corner.

Acknowledgement

I want to thank everyone who has supported me and encouraged me throughout the many years it took for me to write this book. It was a long journey, but they were there to cheer me on and see to it that I didn't give up.

I have no doubt that without them, this book would have never come to fruition. I owe them all my deepest gratitude. Especially my mom and great-aunt Jo.

Thank you all.

Table of Contents

Chapter 1

ONE SHORT, ONE LONG

The motorcycle roared into the country store's dirt lot, raising a cloud of dust, too thick to see its rider. A couple of the older gentlemen standing around were so startled by its sudden arrival that one ran for the store's front door, and the other dropped his pipe trying to follow. The presence of the bike was about as welcome as a freight train running through your backyard. It was loud, frightening, and extremely out of place.

It wasn't uncommon to see motorcycles on the mountain, but they never stopped on their way through. The nearest gas station was several miles back down the road, so they always had filled up and drove on through; they never seemed to notice there was actually a town here. Granted, the country store tripled as a store/Post Office/fire station (with the fire truck parked around back), but no one ever stopped to ask why there were people this far up the mountain. The population was thin—just eighteen—but, then again, so was the air.

The motorcycle came to a halt a few feet from the store's front porch, which also turned out to be just inches from ol' man Warner's pipe. He didn't dare reach for it; instead, he backed up and leaned against the door of his rusted, green pickup. As far as everyone in Knicker's Notch was concerned, ol' man Warner ran the place, but not at this moment. He preferred to be just an innocent bystander for the time being, and it was surprising to see him being so timid around a stranger. 40 Jake Warner, in his 40 years on Castleback Mountain, had seen it all. He was a gentle but outspoken old man in his mid-sixties who always wore Osh Kosh overalls and never went anywhere without his pipe.

The mysterious visitor gave ol' man Warner a friendly nod as he shut off the bike's engine and engaged the kickstand. ol' man Warner nodded back, although it seemed more of a nod of relief than one to compliment the one, he'd just received. He was relieved that neither he nor his pipe had been run down in the scuffle. The rider dismounted, never taking his eyes off his observer. He read Mr. Warner's mind, for no sooner had he dismounted the bike than he bent over and retrieved the pipe. He brushed it off, looked it over to ensure it was okay, then handed it to its owner. "Sorry 'bout that, sir," he said, sheepishly, "didn't mean to scare ya'."

Mr. Warner took the pipe and stuffed it, as well as his hands, into his pockets. "That's alright, son," he answered, "we're just not used to those damn things up here. Don't see 'em often enough, that's all."

The stranger removed his dark glasses and squinted in the mid-morning sun. He glanced around the tiny square while Mr. Burroughs, Warner's gossip partner, emerged from the store. He joined Warner.

"Don't suppose you could tell me where the police station is, could you?" The stranger asked, putting his glasses back on.

"Sure can," Burroughs piped up, "right inside the store, there."

"Is there some sort of trouble?" Warner asked, leaning forward a bit with curiosity.

"No, none at all," the man answered, "just have some business to tend to."

He left the two of them there to wonder just what that 'business might be. As soon as he was out of earshot, ol' man Warner lit his pipe.

"That's a very strange man, there, Warn. What do you think?"

"Me?" Warner replied, "What do I think?"

"Yeah," Burroughs repeated, "Don't ya' think he's a little odd?"

"I dunno," Warner sighed, "I do know that I like those shitkickers he's wearin'."

"Ya' mean those dumb lookin' cowboy boots? Bet they cost him some money."

"I'll bet he can afford 'em, too," Warner said, puffing on his pipe. "Jes' look at this machine he rode in on."

The two men were walking circles around the motorcycle in awe when the stranger returned.

"I thought you told me there was a police station in there," he said, obviously irritated.

"Oh, well, we don't have a police station, exactly," explained Warner. "If there's a problem, you just tell Warren in there behind the counter. If he thinks it's serious or a crime, he'll call the State Police."

"You don't have a police station?" the stranger asked in amazement.

"Sir," Burroughs cut in, "there's only eighteen residents here in Knicker's Notch. We don't need a police station."

"The size of a community dictates the number of law enforcement personnel needed," the man stated, matter-of-factly, "but every community needs law enforcement, regardless of its size."

"Good Lord, man!" Warner exclaimed, "Where did ya' ever hear that bunch 'a crap?"

"It's not crap," he replied angrily, "and I heard it as a student at the Police Academy."

"Oh shit," Burroughs muttered, shuffling the dirt under his feet.

"You're a cop?" Warner asked.

"Yes, sir," he replied, standing straight, "and proud to have been one for the last eight years."

"Well, I'm Jake Warner," he said, extending his hand, "a resident of this, here, Knicker's Notch for the last 40 years. Sorry if I offended you, mister..." "Doyle. Trevor Doyle," he answered, shaking Warner's hand.

"Mister Doyle. Sorry 'bout that if I did, but I still think that's bullshit."

Warner returned the stranger's smug look, while Burroughs kicked more dirt around.

Lawerence Burroughs, formerly an obstetrician, is a nosy but very nervous man. His wife, Marge, insists that twenty-eight years around "all those nervous fathers-to-be" made him that way. He's great with children, but around adults he's very quiet and well-reserved.

At this particular moment, there could've been no hole large enough for him to crawl into. He was all too aware that his buddy, Warn, had just offended a police officer. He was also very embarrassed that he was present when it happened. He knew Warner was enjoying this showdown, and he wanted to leave.

"Mr. Doyle, Warner continued," in my 36 time here, there has never been any crime. At least, not what you might call a crime. We've had some problems with some of the people passing through, being drunk and belligerent, but no rapes or murders or anything of that nature. We have no need for law enforcement, 'cause no one breaks the law."

"Aren't you afraid someone might?" asked Doyle. "What if someone robs this store or breaks into your house while you're gone?"

No, I'm not afraid, Warner replied. "Warren never has a lot of money in there, and my wife. Elsie knows how to use the shotgun."

Doyle shook his head and looked around for a moment. "Well, sir," he said, "I'm scared. My wife and I just bought the old Rupert place down the road. I'd like to know who's gonna look out for her."

Warner looked at Burroughs, smiled, then back at Doyle again. "Well," he replied, "I reckon you will. You're the police officer, aren't ya'?"

"I don't believe this," Doyle murmured. "Look, Warner said," "if it'd make ya feel better, I can call a town meeting, and we can all talk 'bout this. How's that?"

"That sounds fine to me. When?"

"Burr, go tell Warren we wanna have a town meeting, will ya' please?"

"Sure thing, Warn," Burroughs answered, excusing himself and disappearing inside the store.

"Mr. Warner," Doyle said politely, "when do you think you'll have this meet..."

The rest of Doyle's words were drowned out by the ear-piercing blast of the fire horn. The first blast was short, but the second lasted nearly ten seconds.

"Right now," Warner answered when the horn had stopped blaring. "One short followed by one long means a meetin'. Two shorts every five seconds or so is a fire. Three long means bad weather, and one lets everyone know it's high noon. Got it?"

"NO."

"Well, it'll take a while. You just moved here. but you'll get used to it."

Warner relit his pipe, then wandered over to take a seat on the steps of the store. Burroughs joined him and sipped a can of beer.

"Warn, are you sure this is such a hot idea?" He whispered, not wanting the stranger to hear.

"I don't see any harm in it. Burr, Besides, look at him pacing over there. He's not gonna let this thing rest 'til we take care of it somehow."

Burroughs eyeballed the man before he answered.

"Maybe you're right."

"Burr," Warner said. Turning to face his friend, "You know, I always know what's best 'round here, and..."

"I know, Warn," Burroughs interrupted, "You've been up here over 40 years, and you know everything 'bout everything. Even where the sun sets on the mountain."

"Damn right. I do."

The two men sat in silence, waiting for the rest of the town to arrive.

Chapter 2

TOWN MEETING

The first to arrive for the town meeting was Warner's wife, Elsie. She and Jake lived less than a mile from the store, so she was on foot.

"I'll be damned," Warner said, "She's usually the last to get off her duff and get down here."

"Warn, be nice," Burroughs scolded, "there's a stranger present."

"That's my wife!" Warner yelled to Doyle.

"Why didn't you come n' get me? Jake?" She called, rather upset.

"You got two good legs, he replied, relighting his pipe.

"Warn," Burroughs protested.

"Stow it. Burr."

Elsie was carrying a glass of lemonade and wearing her "meeting dress." It was a special dress she wore only to town meetings. Elsie felt that she should look extra nice, as her husband was the self-appointed chairman of these meetings. Jake actually hated the dress but didn't dare tell his wife that.

"Who's that man?" she asked when she'd gotten closer.

"Jes' wait 'til everyone gets here, Warner said, and I'll explain everything then."

Next within walking distance was Andy Pierce and his wife, Diane. Their two-year-old, Nicholas, came running up the hill first. Diane was jogging behind him, trying to keep up. "Nicholas Andrew Pierce!" she screamed, "Come back here, now!"

"Toda, toda, toda!" he was yelling, ignoring her.

Everyone laughed as little Nicholas ran up to Elsie and pointed to her glass. "Toda, toda," he said again.

"Hi Nicky," she greeted, "No, this isn't soda. It's lemonade, honey. Would you like some?"

"Yeah!" Nicholas answered, jumping up and down.

"Can he have some, Di?" Elsie called.

"Sure," Diane answered, slowing down to catch her breath. "Go ahead, Nicky, it's o.k."

Elsie bent over and handed the glass to Nicholas, who promptly took it and drained its contents.

One by one the rest arrived: Andy Pierce, finally, wandered into the tiny square, followed by John Melbourne riding his new, 12-speed Schwinn bicycle. He was followed by the newlyweds, Mike and Sharon Cummings, also fairly new to Knicker's Notch. Next came the Mitchells—George and Miriam. They were on foot and waved to their son, Pete, as he drove by in his van. Inside were his wife and daughter, Linda and Elizabeth, respectively. Marge Burroughs came barreling over the hill in her station wagon, paying little attention to her driving and chatting with Warren's wife, Marlene, in the passenger seat. Warner began greeting each as they arrived, while Burroughs jumped up and went to see his wife. He could be heard giving her hell for driving like a fool... She was saved by Mr. Warner, calling to order the informal (or formal, depending upon your point of view) gathering.

"Alright everybody," he yelled from the porch, "let's get this meetin' goin'."

"Wait a minute!" Doyle called out, "We can't start yet. I only count seventeen here, not including me. Didn't you say there were eighteen?"

"Abner," someone murmured.

"Who?" Doyle asked, looking around for the person who'd spoken.

"Abner, Andy piped up," "Hey, John, where the hell is Abner?"

"Damned if I know," he answered, stomping out his cigarette in the dirt. "You know him...he does what he wants, where he wants, and in anyone's yard."

Laughter rolled its way through the group.

"AAAAABNER!" Warner yelled, cupping his hands around his mouth. "Oh, AAABNER! WHEERRE AAAARE YOOOOU?"

Everyone looked around, waiting for the long-lost soul to arrive. It was Nicholas who spotted him first, breaking away from the grip his mother had on his hand and running down the hill. "EEEEEEEH!" he was screaming as he vented.

Everyone applauded as Abner, everyone's favorite St. Bernard, came bounding over the crest of the hill, slobbering and barking.

"Wait one, damn minute, Jake!" Doyle called, "HE'S the eighteenth?"

"Sure is." Warner answered, that smug expression all over his face, again.

"You can't count him in, Doyle argued."

"Why the hell not? He DOES live here, doesn't he?"

Warner lit his pipe and waited for Doyle to answer. He did, but he muttered so softly, no one heard him.

"Alright, then," Jake continued, "This man, here, is Trevor Doyle. He and his wife...?"

"Megan," Doyle interjected.

"Megan," Warner went on, "just moved into the ol' Rupert place. I'm sure you'll have time after the meetin' and in the days ta' come, to introduce yer'selves, so I won't waste yer' time with doin' that shit myself."

"Jake, watch your mouth, " Elsie prodded from behind. There were some stifled giggles amongst the group. which made Elsie blush and Warner roll his eyes.

"As I was sayin'," he went on, "Mister Doyle just moved here, and he's a little concerned 'bout the fact we have no police department. See, he's a policeman and used to havin' laws enforced and all of that."

"We don't need any police," George Mitchell called from the back. "There's not enough people here to warrant it. no pun intended."

"That's what I told him," Warner said, "still he thinks it's important for the welfare of his wife, as well as the rest of us, to have it."

"Excuse me, sir," Doyle said, climbing the steps to join Warner, "may I speak for myself?"

"Be my guest," Jake replied, stepping aside.

Trevor Doyle cleared his throat and donned a serious, professional look, aware that his words would have to be impressive if he were going to convince these folks of his sincerity.

Trevor Doyle, at thirty-two, looked more like a basketball player. He was a solid six feet three and well-built. Ironically, that had been Trevor's dream—to play pro basketball, but he failed to get the scholarship he needed in high school. He opted to go to the Police Academy instead, as he'd always admired police officers. It turned out to be the best decision he could've made. In the years that followed, he realized that being a cop was far more rewarding than being a ballplayer ever could've been.

"Good morning everyone," he began, removing his sunglasses. "As Mister Warner just explained, my wife and I just moved into town, and I'm concerned that you have no police department. You all say there's no need to have one. 'cause no one's breakin' the law, but isn't it better to be safe than sorr'y? My wife, for instance, is eight months pregnant. Who am I going to call for help if she goes into labor in the middle of the night?"

"Well," Andy spoke up, "we got that problem solved. Mr. Burroughs is an obstetrician".

"I guess that's good to know," Doyle conceded, smiling at Burroughs, "but I'd like to point out that Mister Burroughs is breakin' the law, even as we speak."

"What?" Burroughs snapped, angry at having been singled out.

"I'm sorry, sir," Trevor explained, "but you're breakin' the open container law by drinking in public."

Burroughs glanced at the beer can in his hand, then up at his wife, Marge, who was just as shocked as he was. He immediately wandered over to the trash barrel and disposed of the can, rejoining the group but avoiding eye contact.

"Mister Doyle," Warner said, stepping up beside him, "don't ya' think you're bein' a bit ridiculous?"

"No, sir, I don't. You folks say there's no need for law enforcement because no one breaks the law. Well, I was just pointing out that you're wrong."

There was some discussion in the group, which told Trevor he was gaining ground. "I'd like to illustrate my point further, if you don't mind," he continued...

There was no response. All eyes were on him, waiting for him to continue, though.

"Dear ol Abner, here, seems to be on the loose all the time, right?" Doyle asked no one in particular.

"Yeah," John answered, Abner's owner. "What's the problem with that?"

"Well," Trevor replied, "doesn't it bother anybody that he's always defecating in their yard?"

"Defa-what?" John asked, confused.

"Defecating," Doyle repeated.

"What the hell does that mean?" Jake asked.

"Taking shit," Doyle said, flatly.

That point struck a familiar chord, as every head in the group nodded.

"Yeah," George Mitchell answered. "I've stepped in it more times than I can count. I'm gettin' pretty darn sick of it, too."

"Me, too," Elsie Warner chimed in. "Every time I go out to hang my wash, there's a fresh pile underfoot."

"He's ALWAYS doin' it in my barn," Jake added quietly.

"Well," Doyle continued, "there's such a thing as a leash law, which can prevent that from happening."

More discussion between the group members. This time, Trevor knew he'd convinced many of them that there WAS a need for "law enforcement"—even to take care of the not-so-serious problems. He wondered if he should give them another example but decided not to. He didn't want to alienate too many of the folks by pointing out they were breaking the law.

"Let's take a vote," Warner suggested. "Those in favor of hirin' Mister Doyle as our policeman, raise your hand."

Every hand went up, except for Warren Corbett's, the store's owner.

"What's yer' problem? Warren." Jake asked.

"I jes don't like the idea, that's all," he replied. "and why not?" Jake inquired. "You should be happy, ownin' the store and all."

"I am," Warren agreed, "but I'm not."

"Stop talkin' circles, Warren," Marlene scolded. She hated it when her husband did that. "What's the problem now?"

Marlene already knew. It was his pride. For the last 36 years, he'd run the store, and it was his job to decide when to call in the State Police. It made him feel important, and now, this stranger was going to take that away from him.

"We don't need it," he snapped, "and we sure can't pay for it."

"Warren, that's a crock, and you know it," Warner shot back. "We make enough from the tourists going through to bring in the National Guard, for Chris's sake."

That was true. Knicker's Notch saw a lot of people during the winter months, who HAD to pass through, on their way up to the ski trails. Warren never increased his prices to take advantage of their business. He didn't have to. They sold a lot of homemade jellies and such, in addition to the usual stuff, and that always attracted the souvenir hunters. The residents didn't pay taxes—it wasn't necessary. They made enough money from sales at the store to cover any expenses the town incurred, and that money was needed so rarely that it sat in the bank, year to year, gathering interest.

Knicker's Notch was the richest town in the state of Vermont.

"Warren. " Jake said, trying to calm himself, "We have lots of money. We CAN afford to hire Mister Doyle, and we CAN afford to pay for whatever stuff he needs to do his job. You're outnumbered, Warren."

Warren was so disgusted, he stormed up the steps past Warner—glaring at him—and disappeared inside the store. Marlene followed, giving Warner the same "you-just-wait" look. Doyle suddenly realized that this idea was not such a good one after all. He intended to help these people. What he'd just done, however, was the opposite—he'd created bad feelings between very old friends.

"Mister Doyle, you're hired," Warner said, extending his hand. "Congratulations, and welcome to Knicker's Notch. You get what you need to make yerself look official and all, and we'll pick up the bill. Maybe it's time we had a police department." Warner shook Doyle's hand and, leaning closer, whispered, "I still think this is bullshit." Then he grinned.

Doyle's jaw dropped. He realized, instantly, that Jake was doing this to save face and look good. It infuriated him. He was being used as a showpiece. Before he could respond, Warner had descended the steps and was mingling with the group. Elsie smiled and followed her husband down the steps.

Andy and Diane approached and shook hands with Trevor, introducing themselves and extending their best wishes. They located their grass-stained toddler, who was busy playing with Abner, and headed off down the hill towards home.

One by one, they all left. Eventually, the only souls left were Trevor and Abner, who was sitting faithfully at the foot of the stairs, wagging his tail and waiting for Doyle's attention.

"Terrific," Trevor observed. "I always wanted to have a K-9 unit."

Chapter 3

TREVOR'S FIRST CALL

Trevor eyeballed the Chevy Blazer for close to thirty minutes before making the decision to buy it. It was only two years old, so the usual fears of buying a used vehicle didn't exist. The color was perfect—black—and the price didn't matter. Knicker's Notch would be the one, as Mr. Warner had said, who would be "picking up the bill."

Trevor wasn't stupid, though. Many times in the past, he'd believed what he'd been told and found himself in trouble for doing so. He wasn't about to purchase what the town couldn't afford, so he'd made some phone calls and had some old friends do some checking. He hated to be so sneaky, but Warner was —or so it seemed—and it was better to be sure before he went shopping.

Once he'd had confirmation that Knicker's Notch had the funds necessary to establish and run a police department, he drew up a set of plans that included the worst-case scenarios, that being, that the town fired him in a matter of months or refused to pay as promised. He wanted to run an efficient operation, but he wanted to do so in a way that would leave little room for mistakes. He knew that Warner would be waiting for the first one so as to make the argument, again, that it wasn't necessary.

He wasn't going to spend more than was absolutely necessary, and what he did spend it on would have to make sense. Case in point: the Chevy Blazer.

He could have bought a vehicle and had it custom-fit with all the gadgets a cruiser holds.

Again, he had to ask that question, though: what if they fire me or refuse to pay for it? He had no contract yet, nor did he have anything on paper authorizing him to buy the necessary items for the town. If the worst happened, he'd be up to his eyeteeth in debt and in possession of a bunch of stuff he had no use for.

He knew the Blazer would be ideal for the terrain. and nasty weather the mountain would see come winter. The need for a four-wheel-drive vehicle was obvious. He knew that no one would argue that point. He owned a CB and had a two-way radio at home. A phone call to his house, and his wife could reach him easily.

He purchased a blue light, which could be easily mounted on the dashboard or roof, and he'd had the town's name painted on the doors. Nothing fancy, but enough to identify the vehicle as official.

He owned three handguns and a shotgun, so arming himself was easily done, at no cost to the town.

He assembled a variety of other items, including a first aid kit. He was a certified EMT, so Trevor's kit was rather extensive in what it contained. He'd carefully packed the rear of the Blazer with other items, including blankets, water, a fire extinguisher, a toolbox with you-name-it, a new car battery (for the soul he ran across who had a dead one—too many jump starts off his could drain it, so he could simply install the extra for the unfortunate person), extra ammunition, antifreeze, and a change of clothes for himself.

It took less than three days to find and fit his police vehicle. He'd brought it home and kept it in the garage until he'd equipped it so no one could see it until he was ready.

Saturday afternoon seemed like a good time to show it off. Trevor was sure that Mr. Warner would be up at Warren's store, hanging around. He went over the Blazer one more time, admiring it and double-checking that everything looked right. He left Megan a note on the table and headed out.

The stretch of road that led to the store was a 1 1/2 mile upward climb. The road, though paved, was beginning to show signs of age—here and there, it bore cracks and even a few potholes. Doyle made a mental note to mention that to Warner. It would need to be taken care of before the winter came and added to the damage.

He reached inside his jacket to make sure he'd remembered the list and receipts for what he'd purchased. The sooner he submitted it to the town, the better. It may take Warner a little longer than necessary to take care of the charges, and he'd dipped into his savings for some of the items he was unable to charge. He smiled to himself when he thought of how Warner would react to the bills. Trevor was certain that he wouldn't have anticipated the purchase of the Blazer on the list of materials. He went over the proper procedures for CPR, just in case Warner's reaction resulted in cardiac arrest.

He was surprised and a tad bit disappointed to find Warner's truck not in front of the store when he reached the crest of the hill. Rather than stop, he continued past and drove up to Warner's place. The road took a sharp curve. just after the store, and when he rounded it, he slammed on his brakes. "Oh shit!" Trevor yelled.

Abner was out for an afternoon stroll, doing so in the middle of the road.

He didn't even flinch when Trevor came to a halt, barely five feet from him. He stopped in his tracks and wagged his tail instead.

Trevor added two more things to his list of things to take care of: a sign for that sharp curve and a leash for Abner. He watched the crazy canine begin to wander around to the driver's side...as slowly as he'd ever seen ANYONE—human or animal—move before. Abner wasn't in any hurry, nor was he in the mood to socialize. Trevor watched in the rear-view mirror for Abner's reappearance behind the Blazer. He didn't want to move until he was sure the elephant-sized furball was safely out of the way. Trevor wasn't sure, however, if he was concerned about Abner being hurt—he knew that with a dog that big, it was possible the Blazer might sustain the more serious injuries. He waited and waited, and still, he didn't see Abner. Trevor changed his glance to the right side mirror, but still, no Abner. "What the hell?" Trevor muttered, glancing to the driver's side mirror, "Where did he...?"

His eyes almost popped clear out of his head. Abner had paused for a moment to "water" the back tire of the truck.

"Thanks a lot, Buddy," Doyle muttered, rolling down the window and sticking his head out". I hope ya feel better, he added, as Abner resumed his stroll down the road.

Trevor put the truck back in "D" and continued on towards Warner's house.

Warner's old green pickup was parked under an oak tree, midway between the house and the barn. Trevor didn't actually see it at first, as all three—the truck, house, and barn—were painted the same color. EXACTLY the same color. He noticed the oak first. It was showing signs of autumn—leaves beginning to change. The tree itself was enormous. "Thank God I don't have to rake this yard," he remarked, pulling the Blazer up behind the pickup.

He wouldn't have heard the beginning of Warner's tirade if his window weren't still open. The first bunch of words was sprinkled with expletives and yelled from the barn. "Oh, oh, Trevor said, climbing out of the truck. He wandered cautiously to the open door of the barn, where he stood to catch his breath. He was already sweating and foreseeing this scene, ending with Warner chasing him out of town with a pitchfork."

"...I don't ba-leeeve this!" Warner was screaming. waving his arms. "I don't know who the hell he thinks he is! He's..".

"Mister Warner?" Doyle interrupted, not moving from the doorway.

"Do you?" Warner continued, redirecting his anger from the chickens to Doyle. "Do you? Just who the hell does he..."

"Calm down," Doyle said. "We can talk about this."

"Talk!" he spat back, "Talk?"

"Yes," Doyle repeated. "You don't have to get so bent outta shape over this. It's just..."

"I don't want to talk!" he screamed, moving towards the door. Trevor took a couple of steps backward. "I am gonna shoot that son-of-a..."

"Over this?" Trevor asked. "It's only a truck, for Pete's sake."

"Huh?" Warner grunted, confused. "What are you talkin' 'bout? I'm gonna shoot that dog for shittin' in my barn for the millionth time..."

Warner glanced over Trevor's shoulder and, SEEING the BLAZER, his jaw hit the driveway. "After I shoot the dog, you're next," he said with a grin.

Elsie Warner set her cup of tea down on the lamp table and moved toward the living room window. She pulled the curtain aside to see where her husband was now. It was odd that Jake's tantrum had suddenly stopped and even stranger that it had lasted only a minute or so. Jake did not throw tantrums often, but when he did, Elsie had learned years ago to just let him throw it. Nothing—no words of comfort or support—could calm him down. All one could do was let him scream and yell and get it out of his system. She'd tried everything over the years to cool him off, including a full blast of cold water from her garden hose, and it failed.

Something had succeeded in stopping him now, and she wanted to know what or who it was. Her eyes fell on the door of the strange vehicle in her driveway. She couldn't read the white lettering without her specs, so she hurried to the lamp table to retrieve them. She fumbled with them, and after adjusting them properly, she returned to the window and pulled back the curtain again. "KNICKER'S NOTCH POLICE DEPT.," she read aloud. "Knicker's Notch Po…" she repeated, the words not registering in her mind. It took a few seconds, but when they did, she gasped and dashed for the phone.

Elsie had a tendency to overreact, and combined with her tendency to act without thinking, it was always a recipe for disaster.

Elsie Warner was about to whip up a Blue Ribbon-winning mess, and nearly everyone would get a taste, too.

Even dear ol' Abner.

Chapter 4

THE ONE THING ELSIE FORGOT

Dispatcher Stephanie Wilson held the receiver at a safe eight inches away from her ear.

"Who the hell is that?" Sgt. Morrow asked. leaning in the doorway. He could hear the woman shouting where he stood.

Stephanie covered the mouthpiece and answered, "I don't have a clue. She hasn't stopped screaming long enough for me to ask".

"Any idea what her problem is?" he asked, coming over and leaning over the counter.

"So far," Stephanie began,"she's told me nothing that makes any sense. She started off yelling that the neighbor's bleeping dog bleeped in the barn again, and her husband was just upset." Stephanie glanced at the notepad she'd been scribbling on. "She's been sayin' something about the new guy in town playing policeman and that he's in the driveway arresting her husband. "

"Anything else? Like where she's calling from or who she is?" "Nope. She keeps repeating the same basic stuff. again. Correction. She keeps screaming the same thing, and each time she adds a few more curses."

"Let me see if I can calm her down," he offered. trying not to smile too broadly. Stephanie surrendered the phone gladly.

"M'am?" He greeted, "Calm down, this is Sergeant Morrow. Can I help you?"

He listened to her repeat the story he'd just heard from Stephanie. "Listen," he interrupted, "I need to know who you are and where you are so I can send a cruiser up to help you."

Stephanie watched him roll his eyes and understood why when he leaned over and scribbled something on her notepad: "Knicker's Notch."

"Uh huh," he acknowledged, "I see. Can you hold second, please? Thanks" for Stephanie took the cue and pushed the red button. on the phone.

"I don't know," Morrow concluded, "whether she's serious or bonkers."

"Who is it?" Stephanie asked.

"Jake Warner's wife," he answered.

"Has she got her meeting dress on?" she asked, smiling.

"How'd you hear about that?" Morrow replied. "Gossip in the coffee room," she answered.

"Oh," he said. He glanced at the board on the wall to remind himself what officers were on duty. "Get David on the radio and tell him to call the station. Not on the radio, the phone. I don't want the entire world to know what's up."

"You want to talk to him when he phones in?" Stephanie asked, turning towards the radio.

"Yes," Morrow answered, "and don't give him any info over the radio. If he knows he's gonna go up the hill, he'll get himself conveniently lost."

"And what shall we tell Mrs. Warner?" Stephanie inquired.

"Tell her to stay calm, that help is on the way," he replied. "I'll take David's call in my office."

Stephanie picked up the radio call mike and was about to transmit when she noticed the light on the phone go out. "Oh, oh," she said, "looks like she ain't gonna wait for the cavalry to rescue her."

"Find David and tell him to get up there," Morrow ordered, changing his mind. "Unfortunately, by sending this one out over the radio, he won't be the only one going, though."

"You going, too?" she asked. Stephanie couldn't resist adding, "No need to get your 'knickers in a twist, too."

She grinned as wide as possible, proud of her little play on words. Morrow rolled his eyes and headed for the door. He turned and greeted her smile by crossing his eyes.

"Someone has to be up there to unravel that twist, M'am," he answered.

Elsie wasn't going to wait. She knew they had enough information, and she couldn't just wait on "HOLD."

She stood in the kitchen for a minute, trying to decide what to do next. She couldn't just let Jake get arrested. He hadn't done anything, except vent some steam and use a few bad words. Now, that hot-shot know-it-all was going to arrest him. She had to help Jake. She had to do something. Anything but stand there like a...

That's when she remembered.

She scurried down the hall and yanked open the hall closet door. It wasn't there. "Oh, Jake," she said. "I should know by now; you never put things where they belong."

She hurried back down the hall to the kitchen and checked the back porch. Not there. Behind the fridge? Not there either. She opened up the broom closet, and there it was. Jake's shotgun.

She didn't check to see if it was loaded, as Jake always kept it that way. Besides, the mere sight of it should be enough to show that "hot-shot," she meant business.

"Damn, this thing's heavy," she muttered, using both hands to lift it from the closet. She adjusted the shotgun. So she was holding it, barrel pointed down, just as Jake had shown her.

Elsie Warner, armed and rather angry, headed for the front door. She ignored the ringing of the telephone. She'd wasted enough time on it.

"ONE to FOUR, report please, over," Dispatcher Stephanie Wilson called.

Sgt. Morrow removed the gum from his mouth, dropped it in the cruiser's ashtray, and reached for the radio mike.

"ONE this is FOUR," he replied, "go ahead."

"FOUR, this is ONE," Stephanie began, "No answer at the residence at this time. What's your E.T.A.?"

"ONE, this is FOUR," Morrow answered, "keep trying that number. FOUR and NINE are en route and will arrive in two minutes. Stay at ringside; you may need assistance. Over."

"FOUR, this is ONE. Request to monitor the call, acknowledged. Will remain at ringside. Making popcorn as we speak, over".

Sgt. Morrow burst out laughing, ignoring Stephanie's minor violation of transmission procedures. The fact was. Any trip up the mountain to Knicker's Notch to date was like a circus. The State Police were rarely called, but when they were, the problem was minor. Most often it was downright humorous. His first (and last) encounter with Jake Warner had taken place the previous fall. He'd just been assigned to the area, and when the call came in, he thought it would be a good way to introduce himself. He'd already heard that Knicker's Notch was an unusual place, though no one would tell him just why.

He knew how the town worked when it came to law enforcement. They called when they felt they couldn't handle something themselves. On this particular day, the caller merely said they had a problem and would explain when he arrived. The caller refused to explain further, but Morrow determined it wasn't an emergency. They sounded calm, so he took his time getting there. He'd taken the corner after the store in time to see the whole town—Abner included—darting and running all over the place. Traffic coming in the opposite direction was at a standstill, with a dozen cars lined up. The people in those cars were foliage sightseers, returning from their trip up to the summit. Not one of them was occupying their respective vehicles, though.

They had abandoned their cars to help Jake and the rest of the town chase down his pigs.

All sixteen of them.

The larger ones—the adult pigs—weren't the problem.

It was the nine piglets that could not, would not be caught. There were pigs and people everywhere. Morrow couldn't believe it, and at first, he didn't know what to do. He briefly considered calling for assistance, but that was dismissed. He knew that his department would be a prime target for jokes if anyone—especially the paper—got a picture of them chasing pigs. He had no other options. He was there and had to do something.

So...he joined in the chase. One by one, the pigs were caught and returned to Jake's barn, but during the two-hour ordeal, nearly every tourist paused to take in the sight. They also took pictures. Morrow made the paper, and not just the county paper. Someone slipped UPI a shot, so Morrow's mug showed up in papers everywhere.

Although he wished this particular call would turn out to be nothing more than a misunderstanding, something told him it wouldn't be.

Warren Corbett was sweeping off the store's front steps. He was thinking about what he'd said to Elsie when she'd called earlier. He didn't care what was going on over at Jake's. Doyle had replaced him, and, as he told Elsie, if he were arresting Jake, then Jake must've done something wrong. It wasn't his problem. Besides, it sounded rather ludicrous, so he figured Elsie was imagining things.

He finished sweeping the bottom step and was about to ascend them to go back into the store when he heard a car. He turned and watched in shock as two state police cruisers. drove by with their blue lights going.

They were headed for Jake's.

"Oh, oh," Warren, muttered. He dropped his broom and ran inside to call Marlene.

Elsie could hear Jake arguing with Doyle the moment she stepped out on the porch. They were standing in front of the barn, and both trucks were parked between her and them. She descended the stairs and carefully crept around the front end of her husband's pickup, pausing when she got there. As soon as she heard Jake say, "You can't do that," she darted out into the open, pointing the gun at Doyle. She was barely able to hold it at waist level. "Get away from him," she ordered, trying to sound in control.

The sight of Elsie Warner holding a shotgun on him stunned Doyle. He froze, and for a split second, he couldn't believe his eyes.

"Elsie," Warner snapped, "What in hell are you doin'?"

The sight of his wife wielding a shotgun and wearing her apron (which clashed horribly with the dress she had on) amused him. He didn't dare smile, though. He could see she meant business, and laughing at her might upset her more.

"I said get away from him, Mister Doyle," she snapped, taking another step forward. "Are you hard of hearin'?"

"Elsie, put that damn thing down," Warner said.

She was standing a good 25 feet away, and she knew her aim wasn't good, so she started moving forward. The sudden blast of the fire horn startled her, but it was the appearance of the cruisers pulling in the driveway that made her stumble.

The one thing Elsie forgot was you never keep your finger on the trigger.

Chapter 5

BIRDSHOT AND BABIES

No one heard the shotgun go off, except for Elsie. Both Doyle and Warner turned and half-ran, half-stumbled for cover.

Elsie pretty much landed flat on her face in the dirt.

Sgt. Morrow saw the woman with the shotgun and knew it had to be Elsie Warner. He was rounding the corner into the driveway when she fell.

He brought the cruiser to such an abrupt halt that Dave Rawlings, in the cruiser behind him, never had the chance to react.

He slammed into Morrow with such force that the front end crumpled, and he hit his head on the steering wheel. He was knocked out in seconds.

Morrow hit his head just as hard, and although he remained conscious for a few seconds longer than Rawlings, he didn't have the chance to radio in, or react at all.

Doyle felt as if a million needles had hit him, and the pain was excruciating. He stumbled down and landed on the grass, breaking his fall with his knees. He forced himself to roll over, and the second he landed on his back, he knew changing position had been a mistake.

Elsie Warner had just shot him in the ass.

Warren didn't know what else to do. He sounded the fire alarm, thinking that maybe someone else would. The alarm would bring everybody to the store, and when they got there, he'd tell them about the police. He didn't bother to call his wife, because she'd be on her way already.

The system the town had was simple. Instead of having several vehicles converging out front all at once. Three drivers were assigned to pick up the others. Lawrence Burroughs and his wife, Marge, would pick up Marlene. George and Miriam Mitchell would ride in with their son Pete and his wife, and Mike and Sharon Cummings would ride with Andy, his wife Diane, and John Melbourne. Once all arrived, Warren would be out front to tell them where the fire was, and he'd jump in the fire truck. It was, to any outsider, a crazy way to do things, but it had worked on several occasions. Warren would have put a call into the State Police, so additional assistance arrived shortly after.

This time, he didn't call the police for the obvious reasons. They were there already. Although Warren was not aware yet that both cruisers had met their demise in Warner's driveway.

Warren locked the store up and waited on the porch. trying to imagine what it was Jake had done to get himself in such a mess.

Megan Doyle had just returned from shopping when she heard the fire alarm. She counted the blasts to identify for certain it was a fire, then went into the den to listen on the radio. Trevor would probably be radioing her any minute, so she sat down and waited.

She hoped, whatever it was, it wasn't serious and that Trevor would be home soon.

She'd been having contractions now for two hours.

Stephanie let the phone ring another time before hanging up. She didn't like this at all. There was no answer at the Warner residence, and Sgt. Morrow hadn't checked in. She didn't like to bother him, or any officer for that matter, when they first arrived on a scene. Still, it had been ten minutes since he'd arrived, and he hadn't called in to update her. She keyed the microphone and called. "ONE to FOUR," she said, tapping her pen on the desk, "Please acknowledge, over."

She waited about fifteen seconds for a response, then tried again. "ONE to FOUR, come in, please."

"Hey, ONE, whoever ya are, ya' better send up some more cars. These are wrecked; yer friends wrecked em', and they're out cold." There was a pause, then the voice added, "Oh yeah, and we've had a shootin', too."

Stephanie sat in a mixed state of shock and confusion.

"Who am I talking to?" she asked, regaining her composure.

There wasn't any answer.

Jake Warner tossed the microphone back into the cruiser. took a look at the officer slumped over the steering wheel and walked over to his gun-toting spouse.

Doyle was lying on his stomach, moaning, but was barely heard. The chickens in the barn were squawking, and the pigs, now numbering twenty-one, were squealing. Elsie was seated on the ground, where she'd landed, nursing her scrapes and talking to herself.

"Well, my dear, you've done it this time," Jake began. "After the pigs got loose last year, on account 'a you, I thought you'd topped all disasters to date in our years together. But this," he paused to wave his hand across the scene, "this tops 'em all. You've pumped a load of birdshot into one cop's butt and put two cops into comas. You've created a two-car pile-up in our driveway, and somethin' tells me that fire horn had somethin' to do with this, too."

Elsie muttered something, but Jake didn't hear it.

"What's that, Else?"

"I called Warren."

"Oh, Lord' in Heaven," Jake replied, "and he's sounded the fire alarm, which means..."

He didn't finish the sentence because the town fire truck was coming around the corner.

It took Megan Doyle less than a minute to run out the door and jump in her car. Considering she was eight months pregnant and weighing in at two tons (with her clothes off), that was a world record sprint. She heard Jake say something about totaled cars and a shooting and panicked. If it were someone other than Trevor on the radio, then he must be hurt.

She tore out of the driveway and headed up the mountain. She didn't know where Jake lived, but she knew what to look for—signs of trouble. With two totaled cars and everyone in town at the scene, that wouldn't be too hard to find.

She winced again as another contraction began.

Warren brought the fire engine to an abrupt halt alongside the two crumpled cruisers. He had barely finished doing that when Jake was at the driver's side door screaming. "Get this godforsaken thing off my lawn, Warren!" he ordered, waving his arms wildly.

Warren ignored him, opening the door and jumping out.

"Warren, I told you..." Jake warned, taking a step forward.

"Jake Warner," George Mitchell snapped, coming around from the rear of the engine, "What in hell happened here?"

Jake turned to answer him but was cut off by the horrified shout of the one man who could really do anything at the moment.

"Mister Doyle's been shot!" yelled Burroughs, who was kneeling on the grass beside him. "Warn, what in hell did you shoot 'em for?"

"I didn't shoot him," Jake snapped, spinning around and beginning to stomp over towards them.

"If you didn't, George said, then who did?"

Elsie spotted the shotgun lying next to her and began to inch herself away from it. Warren, who was eyeing the rest of the others and their attempts to help the men in the cruisers. saw her and knew instantly.

"Oh my Gawd!" he yelled, "Elsie? How could you? Why did..."

"Stow it. Warren," Jake replied, "This ain't the time to be askin'. We gotta do somethin' about these hurt people and quick! Burr, see what ya' can do. I'll go call the State Police and make sure they're sendin' more help."

Elsie began to get up as Jake headed for the house. He turned on her and pointed directly at her. "Don't you move one inch from where you are," he ordered. "You have done enough."

Elsie realized how angry her spouse was instantly. The last time he'd had that look in his eye had been the day the pigs got loose. She thought it best she not argue. So she sat right back down and folded her arms across her chest. Jake lowered his arm and flashed an approving smile at her knowing how awful and embarrassed she must feel. The smile was to let her know he wasn't going to feed her to the garbage disposal after all this was over.

He turned and began to take the first of the four steps onto the porch, pausing in mid-step. He tilted his head to listen for the sound that seemed to be coming from the direction of the store. It sounded like a car horn. He turned and caught Elsie looking at him and waved her to come over. She was so happy that he was letting her move from that spot that she practically sprouted wings and flew.

"Did you hear something?" Jake asked her when she arrived at his side.

"Like what?" Elsie replied. "There's so much noise, ya' can't hear anythin'."

"I s'pose yer right," Jake agreed, "never mind."

Elsie sat down on the bottom step while Jake headed inside.

It occurred to Jake that the likelihood of it being a car horn was next to none. No one could be blowing one, because everyone in town was in his driveway.

Everyone but Megan, of course, and Abner. Megan had been forced to pull over in front of the store when the last contraction all but blinded her with pain. She knew she was in trouble when, to her horror, her water broke just seconds after shutting off the car.

Abner was wandering around the store's perimeter looking for scraps when Megan pulled in. He ignored the car at first, but even ol Abner understands a woman's cry when he hears it. He bounded over to the station wagon's open window and peered in.

Megan turned her head to find Abner staring at her, and although it startled her at first, she was also thankful to see a friendly face.

"Hi'ya Abner," she half-whispered.

Abner barked his greeting, jumping up and placing his big front paws on the door. His slobbering face was now just inches away from Megan's.

"Do you think you can help me out a little, there, Abner?" she queried.

Abner barked again, as if waiting for his orders.

"Ok buddy, I got somethin' for ya to do for me." Megan told him, "And I hope you can do it fast..."

Jake's front lawn looked like the site of some major disaster exercise, with the exception, of course, that it wasn't just for practice. Everyone was busy doing something, most running around obeying Dr. Burroughs orders. He was the only one who could really do anything, and even that wasn't much. Or, so it seemed, to him. Still, he was bandaging up what he could and trying to make everyone as comfortable as possible. Miriam Mitchell was sitting in the back seat of Dave Rawlings cruiser, reassuring him that things were gonna be ok. Her son Pete, who had some first aid training, was checking him out for broken bones and other injuries. The cruiser that contained Sgt. Morrow was being worked on in an effort to get the driver's side door open. Warren and George were trying to pry it open with crowbars, but it was proving to be a very difficult process. Trevor Doyle was lying on his stomach with a blanket draped over his lower half. It had been placed there once his trousers had been cut away to reveal Elsie's handiwork with the shotgun.

Marlene Corbett had the awesome task of keeping an eye on the children, Elizabeth and Nicholas, while their parents assisted the others. Elizabeth, nearly eight years old, made the task a bit easier, as she entertained Nicholas. She was just old enough to understand that this scene in Mr. Warner's yard was a bad one—like the ones on T.V.—and that Nicholas shouldn't be going near any of it. She had brought her coloring book and crayons with her and managed to persuade little Nicholas to color with her. They were sitting on the grass beside the house, a safe distance from the goings-on in the driveway.

Elsie saw him first. She didn't have her glasses on, but it wasn't difficult to figure out that the brown blob running across the lawn was Abner. He stopped a few feet from the scene in the driveway and looked around. Everyone seemed to be very busy, and he needed to find someone who wasn't. He and Elsie made eye contact at the same time, and he made his way around the chaos to her. He instantly dropped the item in his mouth at Elsie's feet and barked.

"Abner," she greeted, reaching down to see what it was, "What sort of present did you bring me?" She picked the object up and wiped it dry of the contents of Abner's mouth, emitting a "yuk" as she did so. It was a plastic card of some sort, but without her specs, she couldn't read it. Jake was just coming out the door, so she turned and handed it to him. "Jake, what's this?"

"Else, I haven't got time to..." he began to protest, then stopped when he realized what it was. Abner barked twice, as if to explain.

"Jake?" Elsie prodded, "What is it?"

"It's Megan Doyle's Medic-Alert Card," he replied, confused. "Why in... where did Abner get a hold of this?"

Abner barked again, but this time he bounded over to where Trevor was lying on the grass. Jake descended the steps and followed. He knelt down next to Trevor and tried to talk to him. "Doyle," he said, "Abner just found yer' wife's Medic-Alert Card. Where would he get this?"

Trevor groaned, then mumbled something.

"What?" Jake asked, "I didn't hear ya'."

"Where is she?" he demanded.

"I don't know; Abner brought it here."

Trevor thought for a moment, then it came to him.

"Baby," he spat, wincing in pain, "She needs help 'cause she's havin' the baby!"

Jake shot Burroughs a horrified look, and he went sheet-white. "How can you be so sure 'bout that?" Jake asked.

"Jake, damnit," Elsie snapped, "Don't be an old fool!"

She came around to stand behind Burroughs, where she could face him. "Where else would Abner get it? And why not send all medical emergency cards along if you're havin' a medical emergency? For God's sake, Jake, we can't take the chance of not going to see!" She clenched her fists and stomped a foot to underscore her anger.

"Burr," Jake said, "We gotta go find out, and you have to go too. You're the baby mailman 'round here, and if that's what's happenin', you'll have to do the deliverin'."

Burrough's mouth dropped open in shock. "But," he stammered, "What about these others?"

"The police are coming' with help," Jake snapped, "Now get yer butt movin and go! Get Warren to drive you there in the engine."

"But we don't know WHERE she is!" he nearly yelled.

"No," Jake agreed, "But Abner does. Follow the furball, and I'm sure he'll take you right to 'er."

Abner barked his agreement to lead and watched as Dr. Lawerence Burroughs sighed and rose to his feet. Jake and Elsie watched as he went over to speak to Warren, who uttered a loud "NOW!?", then dropped his crowbar (nearly on Burrough's foot) and headed for the fire engine. Jake turned to Elsie, who looked relieved that Jake had sent them out looking. "Thank you," she whispered softly, smiling gratefully.

"You're welcome," he replied, "I may be old, but I'm not a fool. Jes a little slow, at times, is all."

Jake turned his gaze back to the fire engine, now backing out onto the road. He quietly uttered a prayer, thanking the Lord that Burroughs was who he was and that he'd get to Mrs. Doyle in time. He spotted Abner running across the lawn to take up his position as guide and added a promise to his prayer. "And Lord, if you see to it that Burr gets to her in time, I'll let Abner do his thing in my house, if he wants from now on." "Amen."

Jake Warner meant every single word, and he wondered if Abner had somehow heard him, as he suddenly broke into a run down the road, faster than he'd ever run before.

Chapter 6

JAKE'S BIG MISTAKE

Dr. Lawrence Burroughs sat in the front seat of the fire engine reviewing the procedures for delivering a baby. He'd done it dozens of times in his lengthy career, but never under the circumstances he was about to face.

"She picked a helluva time to have a baby," Warren yelled over the sound of the engine accelerating.

"Women don't..." Burroughs began, but he was cut off by the awful sound of Warren grinding the gears when he shifted.

"What?" he asked, completing the action.

"I said, women don't decide when they're gonna have a baby," Burroughs stated, "the baby does, and when it decides it's time, it doesn't care what you're doing."

Warren rolled his eyes in exasperation. The last thing he needed was a speech from Burroughs about babies and' stuff.

"Why did I get elected to go with you?" he asked, shifting again, trying to keep Abner in sight.

"You're the only one who can drive this garbage can," Burrough replied, having doubts already as to the truth of that statement.

"Terrific," Warren announced. "I suppose Jake was the one who chose me, right?"

The fact that Burroughs said nothing was answer enough. Warren made a mental note to "thank" Jake for the honor he'd bestowed on him.

They had just rounded the corner and could see the store coming into view. Abner vas headed straight for it.

"Isn't that the Doyle's station wagon out front there?" Warren asked, pointing in its direction. "She must be in it."

"Pull up right next to it," he said. "I may need some of the first aid stuff from the back, and I want it handy."

Warren nodded and began to slow down to do so. Abner was standing at the driver's side window, barking furiously.

No one but Abner heard Megan whisper, "Thank God," from within. She was all too aware of how close things were. The newest addition to Knicker's Notch was about to arrive in town.

Warren was bringing the truck to a stop when two ambulances and three cruisers soared over the crest of the hill towards Jake's. "There goes the cavalry," he muttered.

Megan Doyle vas so busy concentrating on her predicament and sunk so far down in the seat, she didn't see the parade of emergency vehicles scream past the store toward Jake's. Their sirens were drowned out, somewhat, by the noise of the fire engine Warren was parking behind her car, blocking her view of the road.

She did, however, catch a glimpse of something out of the corner of her eye and turned to the left to get a better look. She saw what appeared to be a helicopter flying towards Jake's, and that's when she knew for sure something was terribly wrong.

Stephanie Wilson had decided to err on the side of caution after that confusing transmission from Jake Warner.

She dug out the phone number of her superior, and upon his orders, she had called out the "cavalry." Including the helicopter from another station. She was relieved when Mr. Warner had finally called her to explain further the details of the disaster in his driveway. The only problem with Jake's version of the story was he neglected to explain to her that the events had all been an accident. She had listened to him explain while recording his words—which was a normal procedure when one called the police. His brief summary went simply like this: "My wife shot the town's police officer, and two of your guys who came up to help got hurt, too. I hope you're sending more help. I have to go now; they're hurt badly. Bye."

Stephanie had held the receiver for a solid minute, unsure of whether she should send more units. She finally decided to radio the lieutenant, on his way up there, to let him know that Elsie Warner was armed. She'd done that, then sat back and lit a cigarette to wait for what was next. She knew this whole thing was bizarre and recalled, with a chuckle, that it was the day of the full moon. It was always like this when there was a full moon, so when the phone rang and she found Jake on the other end, she wasn't surprised. Not at all.

"Yes, Mister Warner," she said calmly, "I remember you." (How could I forget??)

"What can I do for you?"

"We need another ambulance," he yelled, obviously out of breath.

"Sir," Stephanie replied, "there are two on the way. That should be enough, I think." (...unless Elsie let loose with that shotgun again...).

Jake proceeded to explain the imminent delivery of Doyle's new baby and stressed the need for more help.

Stephanie couldn't believe it. In this tiny town, there had been a shooting, a two-car accident, and now, a medical emergency involving the delivery of a baby...somewhere in the vicinity—all of this in the span of an hour and in a town with a population less than that of two dozen.

Impossible, she told herself. Am I imagining all of this, or is this some sick joke being played on me by the guys in the station? But it wasn't. It was real, and she had to deal with it. "Ok, Mister Warner, I'll do what I can. Just calm down." She disconnected him and keyed the radio mike.

"All units headed up the hill, be advised that additional assistance is needed in the area," she began, trying to collect her thoughts. "Wife of wounded officer is in labor and being attended to, but further assistance and transportation will be required. Acknowledge, over."

"ONE, this is SIX," came the reply. "Can you repeat that and explain, please? Over."

Stephanie muttered an obscenity and keyed her mike. "SIX, this is ONE. Is that you, Jack?"

"Yes, it is." The sarcasm in the voice was obvious.

Stephanie had to take a deep breath before she continued, but even that could not prevent her from responding in a way. That was no less than hostile. and complete jackass. Jack was her former husband.

"What is it that is so difficult for you to comprehend?" she asked.

"I asked that you repeat and explain," he snapped.

"For Chris's sake, Jack!!! The wife of one of the injured officers is down the street somewhere from him havin' a baby! She needs help, dammit! Have you got that, you stupid fool?"

By the time she finished screaming the last words into the mike, she was shaking, wishing she'd moved to her mom's in Oregon when the divorce had gone through last year. Either that, she thought, or I should've taken the settlement money and had him killed.

Slowly, too. Very, very slowly.

"ONE, this is Six, he replied calmly, acknowledged. Please radio the hospital and advise we will be en route with her as well as the others. Over."

"SIX, this is ONE, acknowledged."

Stephanie slammed her fist on the desk and took another deep breath. She closed her eyes for a moment to regain her composure. And, like Jake Warner, she uttered a silent prayer. "Dear God, please let him be right in the way when Elsie lets loose again with that shotgun..." Call the hospital. With that, she picked up the phone to call the hospital.

One cruiser took the corner and made a sharp turn, shooting across the lawn diagonally towards the house. The second came straight up the driveway and veered off to the left, coming to a halt next to the two that were damaged. The third went beyond the driveway and came up the lawn to stop just a stone's throw from the porch. The helicopter, flying in from a different direction, swooped over the field behind the house and was now hovering just above it. The ambulances were waiting in the road for the "all clear" signal.

The cruiser doors flew open, in unison, and each occupant jumped out and drew their gun. The lieutenant, riding with one of the officers in the cruiser near the house, pumped a round into his shotgun and stood behind the shelter of the passenger's side door. He'd never seen Elsie Warner, but he assumed it was the woman now standing horrified near the barn door. He set his sights on her.

"Everyone down on the ground, now!" A voice boomed from the hovering helicopter. "Arms and legs spread! Move!"

The first down on the ground was George Mitchell, who'd seen too many scenes like this on T.V. to argue his innocence. The police were not in the mood to discuss the matter, and it was better to simply do as they told you to. Jake, on the other hand, was not as easily coerced, and he'd had enough of all this. He turned to face the cruiser near the house. "Wait one damn minute!" he yelled.

"Get down on the ground!" the voice ordered again. "This is the State Police, and anyone not complying will be placed under arrest!"

Jake hesitated, then turned towards Elsie. "Do what they tell you!" he called to her. She nodded fearfully and slowly lowered herself to the ground. Once Jake was satisfied that she was not going to do something stupid and get herself shot, he did the same. One by one the rest of the others followed.

"Alright," called the voice. "Now, don't anybody move until they're told to do so."

The lieutenant felt compelled to add something to that, so he picked up the radio mike and switched on the speaker. "We know that not all of you are involved in what's happened, he said slowly, "but until we sort this out, we need to protect ourselves and you. Please be patient."

He tossed the microphone back in the car and began to walk across the lawn towards Jake. If he was protesting, chances were it was his house and his wife that had started this mess.

"Are you sure you gotta have this now?" Warren was asking, trying to get Megan comfortable. "The floor of this store ain't the best place to do it."

Megan stifled another scream.

"Shut up, Warren," Burroughs snapped, unfolding a blanket. and draping it over her legs. "I told ya' she doesn't have a choice."

"But..." Warren protested.

"Look," Burroughs interrupted, "I know this isn't the most convenient time and place, and you probably don't have the stomach for this, but it's gonna happen. Her water's broken, and the little one is fighting to get out. Now, either shut up and help, or go wait outside!"

Abner barked in agreement and sat down a few feet behind Warren, now poised on his knees behind Megan's head. "Nobody asked you, Warren muttered, glaring at Abner. "You got me into this mess, you overgrown dustball, and when this is..."

"Warren!"

"Alright, alright," he surrendered, "just hurry it up."

"Mrs. Doyle," Burroughs began, wiping the sweat from his forehead with his shirtsleeve, "I've delivered lots of babies, but doin' it like this in a fist. I'll do the best I can, and we'll get through it, ok?"

"Thank you," she whispered, already worn down by the seemingly endless contractions. She felt better now that she knew she wouldn't be doing this in the front seat of the car by herself. Bhu is also a bit more at ease. now knew Trevor would be alright. Burroughs had told her the gunshot was not fatal and he was ok. He just didn't tell her exactly where he'd been shot. She focuses her attention on the problem at hand.

"Alright, there, Megan," Burroughs said, positioning himself, "Push!"

"You've got helluva nerve comin my property like this! Jake Warner was yelling," We've been helpin these people, and yer' treatin' like common criminals.

Lieutenant Travers spun around and watched back over to the porch, where all of the townspeople, with the exception of Megan, Trevor, Warren, and Burroughs,. and handcuffed. Every single one of them fed. been now seated. handcuffed—they'd all been read their rights. Lt. Travers had been as patient and civilized as possible, but Jake's mouth had managed to get everybody in a heap of trouble. Rather than engage in any more arguments about 'who had what right to do what,' Travere had ordered Jake to sit down on the porch. and keep his mouth shut. He refused. Was he arrested? The others began protesting that action, and Travers decided to just arrest them all and sort it out later. Two more cruisers were en route to begin taking them all to the station.

"Mister Warner," Lt. Travers said, leaning forward. So as to look down upon Jake. "Your wife is criminal. She shot a police officer, and that is a very serious crime." "It was an accident, Jake replied." I already told ya that.

It makes no difference right now. Travers snapped, "I'm doing my job, and that includes arresting whoever has committed a crime, and whether she's guilty or whether or not it was an accident will be up to the court to decide. Do you understand me?"

Jake's face was a wan lobster-red, and he was sweating profusely. Marlene Corbett, seated beside him, noted how worked up he was. "Jake," she urged, "Calm yer'self. You'll work yerself into a heart attack, and that won't do Elsie any good."

Jake turned and kneeled at her. "No, it won't. I know that, but this is all a big mistake."

"And when he finds that out," Harlene said knowingly. "You can have his badge."

"I would strongly urge that you keep your mouth shut, too, ma'am," Travers said.

"Don't talk to me like that. Sonny," Marlene replied, jumping up. I may be a suspect to you, or whatever, but you have no right to speak to me in that way!

"Lady," Travers began, stepping back to put some distance between them. "If I..."

"Officer," Jake interrupted, rising to join them. "Have you bothered to send help down the road to help out Mister Doyle's wife?" Jake figured changing the subject would diffuse the situation.

"What?" Travers answered, thrown off by the question. "Doyle's wife," Jake repeated, "Did you send her any help?"

Warren knew that if Megan screamed one time,

He would lose it. He was cradling her head in his hands, urging her to get on with the business of having this baby. She was punching hard; the tiny veins in her forehead were bulging out, and it seemed like they were getting nowhere.

"Alright!" Burroughs called out from behind the blanket.

"I think just once more oughtta do it! Come on!"

Abner barked, as if to urge Megan into doing what she felt, at this point, was impossible.

"Push, push, push!" Burroughs yelled, and instantly she did, while letting go of another shriek. This one was different, though, as it was a shriek of relief.

"Yeah!" Burroughs exclaimed, "You've done it!"

"Well?" Warren replied, "What is it? Boy or girl, huh?" "Megan?"

Yeah, she sputtered, tears streaming down her bright red cheeks.

"It's a wonderful-looking little hoy! Congratulations!" Dr. Burroughs announced, "Now, just lay still while I do the rest, and then you can see..." "Oh, oh God!" She screamed, interrupting him.

"Burr?" Warren called. "My God, what's wrong? Is she alright?" muttered from behind the blanket.

Megan stifled another scream, biting her lower lip.

"Burr What in hell is wrong?" Warren demanded, Is she gonna die or something?" "Hold on, Warren, Burroughs answered, hesitantly,

"Because here we go again," he answered.

"What?!" Warren yelled, astonished.

"She's having another one." Warren Burroughs announced.

"Just do what you were doin' before, ok?"

Warren didn't answer.

"Warren, just do it! You'll be fine."

No answer

"Warren, for God's sake, answer me." Burroughs ordered, growing impatient.

Warren didn't utter a word. Burroughs peered over the top of the blanket to yell at him, but he saw immediately how futile that would be.

Warren had passed out and sprawled on the floor behind Megan. Abner licking his face, to no avail. "Thanks, Warren," Burroughs muttered under his breath.

Then he ordered Megan to push again.

Lt. Travers looked at Jaks Warner in disbelief. He had completely forgotten about the baby emergency.

"Oh Lord 'n Heaven," Jake said flatly, "You forgot, didn't you?"

Travers spun around and, for the nearest officer, barked out a stream of obscenities and orders before he went. Jake turned to Marlene and shook his head in disgust.

"I wonder how they're doin'," George said from the porch.

Marlene got a hearty laugh, then announced, "Warren can't stand the sight of blood, so I suspect he isn't bein much help at all!"

"Well, Burr knows what he'e doin'," Jake offered hopefully. "I'm sure everythin's workin' out just fine."

He sat back down on the porch, thinking how nice it would be to have his pipe to chew on.

Chapter 7

STEPHANIE STRIKES BACK

"State Police, you are being recorded." Stephanie answered, extinguishing her cigarette in the ashtray,

"How can I help you?" Steph, this is Jack. came the reply, "Just listen. The boss didn't want this going over the radio."

"Alright, what?" She snapped, wishing it'd been anyone but him calling.

"Things got a little out of hand up here," he began.

"Really?" she replied sarcastically. "What? Did ol' Elsie decide to go hunting again?"

"Stephanie!" Jack yelled, angrily, "I'm serious, now, shut up and listen. Mister Marner didn't take too kindly to us showing up in force, and by the time we got things sorted out a bit, we had to arrest everyone."

"What?" Stephanie replied, leaning forward in her chair.

"What do you mean, everyone? EXACTLY HOW MANY did you guys arrest?"

"Sixteen. I think," he answered rather quietly.

"Jeeeesus Jack, whose bright idea was that? Travers?"

"Don't forget this is on tape," he reminded her. Stephanie reached over and switched off the recording equipment before saying another word.

"Jack," she continued, "where are we gonna put them? It's 11, and it's Saturday, suppertime. We'll have to keep them all' until Monday! Are you guys nuts?"

"Look, dammit." Jack shot back, "I didn't make the decision to do it. Travers did. I told him I'd call to give you a bit of a warning and to have you get on the phone to try and reach Willis."

"Willis?" Stephanie nearly screamed. "Willis? You really must be nuts!" You want me to call Justice "What-the-Hell-Day-Is-This" Willis? For what, Jack? "Don't you think things are already beyond control? You bring Willis in, and the next step will be intervention by the Armed Forces and the Supreme Court."

There was a pause, then an audible sigh as Jack tried to regain his composure. Stephanie, meanwhile, was kicking herself again, though not for sticking around after the divorce. This time she was trying to recall the reason she'd married the man in the first place.

"I agree," Jack said slowly, "that Judge Willis is not running with a fully charged battery."

"Got that right," Stephanie snapped, "you might say his front-end alignment is a little off, too."

"The point is," he went on, ignoring her, "that he'll be willing to come in and process these folks' tonight. He's the only one any of us can think of who'll do it. Either that, or we'll have to hold them until Monday."

"Tuesday."

"What?"

"Tuesday," Stephanie corrected him. "Monday is Granger's day at County."

"Then stop your complaining' and get on the phone!" He yelled.

"I'm on it. Have fun, Jack."

With that, she disconnected him and began the search for Judge Willis' number.

Justice Harold T. Willis had spent the last 37 of his 74 years serving on the bench. Prior to that, he'd been a lawyer but hated it. He'd grown tired of being called in to defend some drunken fool who'd obviously done what he was supposed to prove otherwise, and after 11 years of tap dancing around the courtroom in front of a judge, he chose to pursue that seat of honor himself.

The district court was not all that busy, and for the last several years, he'd worked two days a week filling in for Nat Granger when he had to sit at the county. A typical day for Willis began at 8 a.m. and ended just after noontime. The cases were the usual mix of traffic violations and minor disputes involving the use of fists. The only thing he disliked more than being called in on an emergency was the darn hemorrhoids he'd acquired sitting on that bench all these years. Judge Willis was not fully informed as to the nature of his being called in on a Saturday evening. Stephanie had refrained from giving him the complete details, knowing how easily he would get them twisted. Either that or he would refuse to show up. Willis was not prepared for the chaos he found awaiting him when he arrived at the courthouse.

He couldn't remember the last time he'd seen this many police cars and people.

He pulled his beat-up old Lincoln Continental into the space with his name on it and had barely shut off the engine when his car was overtaken by news people.

Someone was even kind enough to open his door for him.

"Judge Willis!" yelled a woman from behind, "Are you going to oversee the Knicker's Notch case?"

"Judge Willis," came another voice, "do you believe the shooting was an accident?"

Willis stopped in his tracks, just six feet from the door, where he'd managed to get so far. He turned to face the small pack of wolves (as he liked to call them). "Shooting?" he asked rather astonished. There hadn't been one in the county in years.

The group surmised rather quickly that the man was not aware of what had transpired up on the mountain.

"Yes, the shooting up in Knicker's Notch," someone offered. "Didn't you know?"

Judge Willis ran his arthritic fingers through the 5 or 6 strands of hair he had and sighed deeply. "No, I didn't." He answered, "But I do now."

Before they could say another word, he turned and went inside.

Lt. Michael Travers was waiting for Judge Millia in the lobby, which had been sealed off by the police in an effort to keep out the media and any other nosey set of eyes and ears. "Judge Willis I..." he Hogan, extending his hand to shake the Master's.

I will see you in my chambers without delay, Millia ordered, stalking past him. He'd passed from being surprised outside, at the news, to irritated now—having not been told the details of this obviously serious matter.

"Yes, sir," Travers replied, "right away." He fell into step behind the judge and waved to the district attorney. Stephen Drewer nodded and followed them into the small office. adjacent to the courtroom. He paused and closed the door behind him.

Willis wandered around the desk and took a seat. He removed his glasses and placed them on the desk, then his jacket, which he draped over the back of the chair.

Travers and Drewer stood a few paces away in front of the desk, awaiting Willis' attention.

"Alright," he said, "what the hell is going on?"

Fifteen minutes later, Willis rose from behind his desk and walked to the file cabinet near the window. He gingerly pulled open the top drawer and removed a bottle of Tylenol.

He brought the bottle over to the desk and resumed his seat. "Get me some water," he ordered no one in particular.

Travers left the room for the water cooler down the hall.

"Stephen," Willis said, obviously overwhelmed by what he'd just heard, "What in God's name are we supposed to do now?"

Drewer came forward and sat in one of three chairs facing the desk. He plopped his slightly overweight frame into it with a thud.

"We'll do anything," he replied, "except screw this up anymore. than they have, sir."

"Stephen," Willis said curtly, "I'm your uncle, so don't call me sir. No need for that stuff around me when we're alone."

He stirred uncomfortably in his seat before going on.

"From what I've been able to surmise, it was an accident. and it just turned into a set of disasters, if you will."

"Culminating with Travers arresting everyone," Willis added, "and that's where it gets sticky."

"Right. We just let them all go, and Jake Warner will be screaming for damages. We did do some damage to his property, and it was a false arrest."

Willis's mind had wandered for a second, so the name Warner uttered didn't register immediately.

"Warner!" he spluttered, when it finally did. "Jake Warner?"

Drewer nodded, surprised at his uncle's outburst.

"Where is he now?" Willis asked.

"Down at the jail, driving them all bonkers."

"Good," he said, with a grin. "They brought it on themselves anyhow."

"Your water, sir." Travers announced, re-entering the room. He set the paper cup on the desk and turned to Drewer. "Well?"

"Well, what?" he replied, rising to face him.

"Well, have you figured out what we're going to do?" Travers snapped, placing his hands on his hips.

"Lieutenant Travers," Willis interrupted, sipping his water before going on, "may I remind you that this mess is of your doing?"

"I only meant..." he began to say.

"And, may I remind you that your department called me in on a very serious matter late on a Saturday afternoon? without being completely forward about what it was I was being called in for?"

Travers chose to remain silent. Drewer, on the other hand, was fighting back the urge to smite.

"Good," Willis said flatly. "Now that we have that clear, I would like to know where you're holding all these INNOCENT people."

"Sir." Travers replied cautiously, "I don't feel they're ALL innocent. Elsie Warner shot a police officer."

"I will be the judge of that, not you. Now where are they? Your station?"

Travers merely nodded.

"Have they all been processed?"

"I believe so."

"Have they been fed? Willis asked, tossing two Tylenol into his mouth and taking a drink."

"Fed?"

"Yes, fed. It is after six o'clock," Willis stated, "and I'm quite sure that none of them had time to pause for a picnic on Mister Warner's lawn, do you?"

"Sir, do you realize what that'll cost to feed them all?" Travers asked, surprised that he'd even suggest it. "If you just release them all, you'll save the town an awful lot of money."

"Mister Traver's," Willis answered, "you will see to it that everyone down there is fed, and the bill will be taken care of by your station's Christmas Fund. NOT the fund for the needy, but the one that pays for that drunken bash you all throw each year down at that club in Burlington. Is that understood?"

Travers nodded and turned to leave.

"Lieutenant?" Willis called.

"Yes, sir?"

"I want them all in this courtroom in two hours. No more than that, and do not utter a word as to their fate. Treat them properly, and for God's sake, keep your temper!"

Travers turned and all but ran out of the office, humiliated and infuriated. The sounds of laughter made the experience that much more of a nightmare. He stormed past the two troopers standing guard at the front doors and, after pushing his way through the group of reporters in the parking lot, got in his cruiser. He had two hours to do the impossible.

If Stephanie had been told at that very moment she would have to endure two more hours of the chaos surrounding her, she would have been in jail for murder. The problem would've been, however, deciding who it was she would kill. Jack's presence in the building was a nightmare, but it was Jake Warner's constant yelling that was giving it color and dimension. She was working on a second pack of cigarettes, a full bladder that she'd ignored for nearly an hour, and trying to sound in control to the woman on the phone. The caller was from Channel 12, and this was not the first time, but the third, she'd called. Stephanie took a deep breath and crushed out another butt. "All I can tell you is everything is under control, and the department will issue a statement later."

"Look, Miss Wilson," the woman replied, "there has been a serious incident, and the public has a right to know. Is it or is it not true that you are holding sixteen of the residents of Knicker's Notch at your station? AND isn't it true that one of them shot another and some of your own officers were hurt?"

"I can neither confirm nor deny..." Stephanie began to say.

"The hell you can't," the woman snapped. "If you won't tell me, then I will find someone who will."

"Good!" Stephanie screeched into the phone, "Now, get the hell off this line!" She slammed the phone into the cradle and snatched it back up almost as quickly, adding, "and have a nice day!"

She slammed it into the cradle again and ran her fingers through her hair. She stood up and decided to try and make it to the ladies' room. She was met in the hall by none other than her favorite ex-husband. "Watch the fort," she ordered. "I gotta pee." She made her way past several other officers who were scurrying around with the tons of paperwork that the recent events had created. She reached the end of the hall and made a left, not even realizing where she was headed. The restrooms were to the right, through a door.

Through the door to the left were the holding cells. Jake Warner's voice met her the second she opened it.

"I want to make a phone call," he called out. "I'm entitled to a phone call!"

Stephanie froze for an instant, and locating the man, she wandered past the officer posted at the desk and straight over to his cell. She stood directly opposite Jake and calmly asked, "You want to what?"

"Make a phone call," he replied, lowering his voice now that they were inches from each other.

"Who on Earth would you call?" She half shrieked, throwing up her arms. "Your wife's in jail here with you, and so is the rest of the town!"

Warner's jaw dropped open, but he didn't say a word. She merely turned and left the room.

There were four cells, and one was large enough to hold nearly all of them. The group was divided up so that most were in the largest, and Elsie was occupying one all by herself.

"Hey Jake," George Mitchell called from the bunk on which he was seated. "Who was that little lady?"

"I dunno," he replied, "the welcoming committee, I guess. She sure ain't from the Civil Liberties Union, though.

Warner turned and cast a glance into the adjacent cell, where Elsie sat in silence. She hadn't said a single word since they'd handcuffed her back at the house. She refused to even talk to him. She sat there instead, occasionally shaking her head and eyeing the remnants of ink on her fingertips.

"Elsie," Jake said, shuffling over to the joining cell bars. "How are you doin'?"

She looked up at him and smiled, then back down again.

"Don't worry," Else, he assured her. "We'll be out of here in a jiffy."

Stephanie stood in the doorway and stared at what little she could see of her desk and the counter in front of it.

"What the...?" she began to ask aloud.

"Judge Willis' orders," Lieutenant Travers replied from behind her, nudging her out of the way. He carried the cardboard box over the counter and set it on the edge, where it appeared to teeter and threaten to fall off. "He said, Got to feed 'em," he explained, and we only have two hours to do it in. McDonald's was the only answer to that problem."

Stephanie stood for a moment trying to find something to say. Travers looked at her and saw for the first time just how ragged she looked. "Well, Stephanie," he said, "the sooner we get this stuff passed out, the sooner we can get these folks' out of here and to the courthouse." He wandered around to the desk in search of something. "Get Jack and a couple of the other guys in here, and they'll help you."

"Lieutenant," she nearly whispered, having somehow regained. some control.

"Yes?" he answered, looking up.

"Come over here for a second, please," she asked, adding a smile as if she were trying to seduce him.

Travers walked around the counter and came to a stop just a foot away.

To him, the second his left foot made contact with the floor was, looking back on it later, the exact same second that Stephanie's right fist made contact with his jaw. The force of the blow was nearly inconceivable to him, coming from a petite lady her size, but Stephanie was enraged.

And Jack had been a darn good teacher in the area of self-defense.

Travers had stumbled off to his right, nearly falling onto the floor, while she turned and left. He regained his balance, and wiping his mouth, he realized he was bleeding. "Damnit," he cursed, shaking his head.

"Oh, Lieutenant," Stephanie called, reappearing in the doorway.

He stared at her in disbelief.

By the way, she added, removing her badge, "I quit."

With that she dropped it and ground it into the linoleum floor. disappearing once again.

Chapter 8

THE DIVERSION

The two-hour deadline, set by Judge Willis, came and went, which only increased the number of news people and nosy locals in the parking lot of the courthouse. Channel 12 had set up their own crew right out front, and the story had been exaggerated beyond belief.

Judge Willis and his nephew had remained in Willis' office, poring over the newly written reports and combing the law books in search of an answer. They had to find a way out of this awful mess and do so to the satisfaction of one and all.

"We're gonna get sued," Drewer muttered for the fortieth time. "We can drop the charges and let them go, but we will get sued. Count on it." He slammed shut one of the half-dozen law books scattered over the desk and stood up.

"Maybe not," Willis said, removing his glasses. "The only problem we're gonna have to deal with is Jake Warner. He will be the one pushing the lawsuit. If we can pacify him, we're home free."

Judge Willis leaned back in his chair and contemplated his options. "Threatening him is out of the question," he continued, "that'll just feed the fire."

"Can't we just ask him to forget the whole thing?" Drewer asked.

Willis burst out laughing. So hard, he felt his dentures. slip and shut his mouth rather quickly. Once he was sure they were still in place, he answered his nephew, who was still shocked by his outburst.

"Stephen," he replied, "Warner ain't like that. Trust me, I know. I've had some run-ins with him over the years."

"Oh," was all Stephen managed to say, wandering over to the window. The crowd was beginning to grow in the parking lot. "The news people will just love this mess," he observed.

Judge Willis didn't hear his nephew. He was turning the events over and over in his mind, trying to think of something—some way—any way out of this disaster.

It only took him a few minutes to figure it out.

"Call Travers and tell him to bring Warner here," he said suddenly, turning in his swivel chair.

Drewer studied his uncle's face for a moment.

"You have an idea?" he finally said, reaching for the phone.

"I sure do," Willis answered, with a grin, "and you'll love it."

"Well, will ya' look who's come to join us?" Jake announced as Stephanie was brought in, in handcuffs. She was ushered over to the cell, directly across from Jake's, and placed inside. Jake wandered to the front of his cell and smiled broadly. "And what did you do, little lady?"

"Jake," Marlene called from behind him, "leave her alone. It ain't your business anyhow."

"Maybe not, he replied, "but I still want to know."

Jake turned back towards Stephanie. He was about to ask her again when the parade of officers began coming in. No one needed to ask what the cardboard boxes contained; McDonald's is a universal smell and easily recognized.

"Dinner time!" Travers announced, filing in last. His lip was three times its normal size, and uttering those two words was painful. He set his box down on the floor in front of Jake's cell and glanced around at the others.

"The sooner you all eat," he said, "the sooner you can be brought to the courthouse."

Jake watched the other officers set their boxes down and leave. "I ain't eatin' that stuff," he said, grimacing. "I hate McDonald's."

"Betcha hate jail, too, there, Mister Warner," Travers replied matter-of-factly.

"What hit you?" He asked, "A truck?"

Stephanie grinned and waved at Jake from her cell.

He burst out laughing, as did the rest of the group.

"It's not funny," Travers snapped, turning and glaring at Stephanie. She was giggling, too.

"It sure as hell is funny," Jake insisted. "I think it's the funniest thing I've seen all day. And you deserved it, I'll bet, too."

Lt. Travers was not one easily provoked, but this had not been a normal day. Jake Warner was pushing him over the edge.

"I would strongly urge that you keep your observations to yourself, Mister Warner," he warned.

"Or what?" Warner asked, "You'll arrest me?"

"He's good at that," sir, Stephanie called out. "You ought to know that by now, huh?"

Everyone was laughing now, and Travers was infuriated.

"Miss Wilson," he began slowly, turning to face her. "I wouldn't push your luck if I were you."

"Well," she replied, grabbing hold of the bars, "you aren't me and don't care."

Jake and the rest of the group applauded and cheered.

"I think you'll go to the courthouse first, Travers decided, moving towards her cell. "You're only going to cause trouble around here."

"You ain't seen nothin' yet," she muttered under her breath.

But Travers didn't hear her.

Drewer let it ring three more times before hanging up.

"No answer," he said, simply.

"What do you mean, there's an answer?" Willis asked.

"There has to be someone at the desk."

"Well, there isn't right now," Stephen replied.

"Keep trying," Willis ordered.

Drewer picked up the receiver and dialed again.

Jack glanced around the room at the desks one more time before heading towards the door. He wanted to be sure he had every last shred of evidence—every piece of paper in the box he now held. He paused at the door, looking up and down the hall to be sure no one was around. Finding it clear, he hurried down the hall towards the men's room.

He suddenly found himself grinning, regardless of the fact that he was doing something illegal. He didn't care. He had jumped at the opportunity to get back at Travers, not thinking once how his actions might get him fired.

Maybe, he thought...but, first, they have to catch me.

He kicked open the bathroom door with his foot, set the box on the floor in front of the toilet, and then locked the door.

He'd heard of burning evidence before, but this had to be the first he'd ever heard of someone flushing it.

Jake Warner looked at Travers, then at Stephanie. "Nice touch," he commented.

Stephanie smiled at Jake. "Well, considering all he's done to you and your friends AND your wife," she replied, "I think it's in very good taste."

Travers was mumbling and trying to wriggle loose from the makeshift bands that they'd tied him up with. The struggle between him and Stephanie had lasted less than a minute, and once she'd managed to get the upper hand, she'd thrown the keys to the cells to Warner and secured the item now stuffed in Traver's mouth to keep him quiet.

Elsie's undies.

"Now what?" George Mitchell asked. "We can't just waltz out. There are other officers out in the hall."

"I took care of that already," Stephanie answered. "I had one phone call, and I used it. If everyone did what they were supposed to, then the front offices should be empty."

"How did you manage that?" George inquired, beginning to smile.

"I told that nosey bimbo from Channel Twelve News that if she got us out of here, she could get the exclusive."

she explained. "Of course, she offered her assistance."

Warner and Mitchell exchanged curious glances.

"She's gonna be out back with her news truck for transportation out of here," Stephanie added.

"Great," George said, "but that still leaves the other cops in the station to stop us."

"They're all rather busy right now." Stephanie went on.

"She got a friend of hers to create a diversion of sorts."

"What sort of diversion can get half a dozen cops to desert their station?" George asked.

"First," Stephanie explained, "they didn't think it was deserted. Travers is here, and there's another officer out front. Second, this town doesn't take too kindly to having the liquor store robbed. It's Biggie."

"Oh my Lord," Marlene muttered, horrified.

"Calm down," Stephanie said. "It's just a diversion, but by the time they realize it, we'll be gone."

"Well, then, let's roll," Jake said, looking around at the others.

"Wait a minute, Jake," Andy said, weaving through from the back of the group. "Do you realize what we're doin'? For God's sake, we're breakin' out of jail! If we get caught...."

"We won't get caught," Jake interrupted him. "If we do what this little lady says, we'll be fine."

"Who are you, anyway?" Andy inquired, "And why are you doing this?"

Stephanie met the stares of everyone, one by one, before answering. "That nutcase over there has had this coming for a looooong time, she answered. "He thinks he's such a hotshot, and he doesn't give a damn about anyone but himself." She paused, took a deep breath, and then went on. "I've seen him mess things up before, but this time he went too far. You folks shouldn't be here, and because of him, I'm in here, too."

"You're wearing a uniform, though," George observed. "So, how did you end up in the slammer?"

"I slugged him." Stephanie said, flatly. "I am, well, WAS the dispatcher until he pushed me too far. I just decided this time I wasn't gonna put up and shut up."

"Oh, so you're the lady I talked to," Jake concluded, grinning. He extended his hand. "It's a pleasure to meet you, ma'am."

Stephanie shook it. "Enough of this stuff, we're wasting time," she added. "Let's go."

They all began to fall in behind Stephanie as she made her way past the cells to the other entrance. Travers began making noises of protest, but, of course, no one cared.

"Don't tell me there's no one there!" Judge Willis snapped at his nephew. "There HAS to be!"

"Well, sir," Stephen concluded humbly, "they're not answering the phone. I've let it ring a thousand times.

Willis pounded his fist on the desk in anger. "Damn that Travers!" he cursed. "Now what in hell is he doing?"

Drewer chose to just keep his mouth shut. He knew his uncle would prefer it that way.

"Who is the dispatcher down there?" he asked.

"I believe that Miss Wilson was on duty today," Drewer answered.

"Well, where is she?" Willis nearly yelled.

"In the bathroom, maybe?" Drewer replied softly.

"Not for this long, she isn't," Willis snapped. "Get yourself down there and find out what in hell is going on!"

Drewer uttered, "Yes, sir," and nearly ran from the office.

No one could've been in the bathroom at that moment. Jack had been tearing up paper and stuffing it in the toilet for only a few minutes when the inevitable happened. On the fourth flush, the toilet made a "burping" noise and decided it had had enough. To Jack's horror, the toilet began to overflow onto the bathroom floor, and he couldn't stop it. The remnants of the records and a variety of other lovely items of all shapes and colors began to wash over his feet and under the door into the hall outside. He tried all the tricks he knew: jiggling the handle, removing the toilet cover and fumbling with the gadgets inside, and plunging. Nothing worked. The toilet kept overflowing. It never occurred to Jack that he could turn off the water by using the valve behind the toilet.

He watched helplessly as the river flowed under the door.

"Damn, I forgot," Stephanie cursed, trying the knob and finding it locked.

"What's the matter?" Warner asked from behind.

"I need the key," she replied, "and my set is in Traver's desk."

"Well, can't ya just go get 'em?" George asked.

"I'll try," she said, "but we don't have much time. The rest of the gang will be figuring out what's up any moment."

"We're gonna get caught," Elsie announced, finally breaking her self-imposed code of silence. "We'll never get out of here without that happening."

"Eise," Jake replied, putting his arm around her. "We have to try. This ain't right. We're not criminals, and we don't belong here."

"He is right, Mrs. Warner," Stephanie added. "If I can get out of here, I can figure out how to prove you didn't do what you did on purpose. Right now, they see you as a criminal. Do you like that?"

Elsie shook her head.

"Alright, then. I'll go try and get my keys, and you folks stay here."

"Where else can I go?" George muttered.

Jake shot George a dirty look, which George simply ignored. Stephanie, meanwhile, made her way through the group and headed for the front offices.

Stephanie stepped into the hallway from the holding area and stopped in her tracks. "What the hell is that?" she asked no one, eyeballing the flow of multi-colored water on the floor. She followed the trail with her eyes to its source: the bathroom. "Oh, terrific," she said, smiling, too, at the mess someone would have to clean up.

The bathroom door suddenly swung open to reveal Jack standing in the doorway. "Steph!" he called, "Thank God, you're here."

"Jack? What happened?"

"I was getting rid of the evidence," he answered.

"Just' like you asked me to."

"You FLUSHED IT?" She half-yelled. "You can't expect the john to swallow that much paper without anything. happening, you idiot!"

"I didn't think..."

"For God's sake, Jack! Shut off the water!"

"How?"

No sooner had he uttered the question than did the answer come to him. "Oh yeah! he exclaimed, turning and wading to the toilet to find the valve. "Got it!" he yelled. Stephanie stood there, shaking her head. Jack reappeared in the doorway, doing the same. He looked at the floor. "Dammit, now what?"

"I don't know!" she screamed back. "I've got them all waiting at the back door, but it's locked. I need the keys. We have to get out of here before..."

"Before you get caught," a voice answered, finishing the sentence.

Stephanie turned to find Drewer standing midway down the main corridor. He waited for the shock of his sudden appearance to wear off before saying anything more.

"Mister Drewer." Stephanie began, wiping the shock off her face by running her hand over it.

"Miss Wilson," he responded, nodding a greeting. "I can only assume, here, that you're doing something illegal, Care to fill me in?"

"Illegal?" she replied, faking surprise. "What are you talking about?"

"I came down here to find out why no one was answering the phone," he explained. "Judge Willis is very angry about that. I walk in to find no one else around but you and whoever it is around the corner, standing in water and discussing what I believe to be the prisoners. Don't think for a moment, Miss Wilson, that I am as stupid as that. To believe you aren't doing something wrong, that is. So, what gives? Where's Travers?"

Stephanie had no idea what to do next, so she merely turned and pointed towards the holding area. Drewer wrinkled his forehead with a questioning look, then wandered down the hall and by her. He opened the door to the holding area, stuck his head in, and after taking in the scene before him, he shut the door and turned around.

Then he burst out laughing. Stephanie looked at Jack, who was just as shocked by his outburst, too. He shrugged his shoulders and shook his head.

It took Brewer a moment or so, but he finally regained his composure. He adjusted his tie, cleared his throat, and looked at Stephanie with a straight face.

"It appears to me. Miss Wilson, you have everything under control here. I suggest you see to it that the phone is manned as soon as possible. After you retrieve your keys and check the back door, please take your assigned position at the desk."

"I, uh, Stephanie replied, trying to believe what Drewer was doing. I can't do that, Sir."

"Why not?"

"I'm a prisoner, too."

She explained how she came to be one, and Drewer fought the urge to laugh again. "I see, he answered. He looked at Jack, who was still standing in the doorway in a puddle of doo-doo and other stuff."

"What were you doing?" Drewer asked, surveying the nasty mess on the floor.

"Flushing, sir," he replied. "Guess the toilet didn't want it."

"My car," Drewer said, flatly.

"What?" Stephanie asked.

"My car, back seat," he said. "It's out back, and on your way. Throw the blanket that's there over it." He issued the order to Jack, who wasted no time in retrieving the box from inside the bathroom. Stephanie took one look at Drewer and broke into a dead run down the hall to Traver's office. No one was needed. Tell her what to do. She'd just gotten the stamp of approval from the one man who could see her sent to jail, should he want that. Stephanie couldn't believe he had just thrown in his two hands to help them pull off their escape.

She rounded the corner into Traver's office and all but leaped over the desk. She yanked open the right, top drawer, where she'd seen Travers put her keys earlier. He had had her booked but brought her to his office for a speech prior to sending her to her cell. She sailed inwardly, now, thinking how Travers was now tied up in that same cell.

She pulled out the keys and ran out of the office down the hall. She heard the phone at the desk begin ringing. She stopped and looked at Drewer, who nodded to her. She turned and ran back up the two doors to where the phone and radio room was.

"Vermont State Police, you are being recorded," she answered, out of breath.

"Miss Wilson?"

Stephanie recognized the voice instantly.

"Yes, sir."

"What's going on?" Judge Willis demanded. "Where have you been, and where is Travers? Has Mister Drewer arrived yet?"

Stephanie looked up at Drewer, who appeared in the doorway. She covered the receiver to speak to him, but he held up his hand to signal she not do so.

"Judge Willis," she answered, "would you like to speak with Mister Drewer?"

"Yes," he answered, obviously irritated.

She held the receiver out to Drewer, who moved towards it reluctantly. He breathed deeply and gathered his thoughts before speaking.

"Stephen?" Willis asked.

"Yes, sir," he acknowledged.

"I want an explanation."

Drewer didn't want to lie to his uncle, yet he could not tell him the truth, either. He had to exercise caution. The call was being recorded, and he was well versed in the laws of evidence and in how much damage it could do. He thought of his answer and slowly began.

"Sir, I just arrived and have found the reason. The phone went unanswered."

"Well?"

"It's kind of crazy down here, sir," Drewer continued. "First of all, Miss Wilson went to use the bathroom, and someone stuffed too much paper in the toilet. It began overflowing, and she was in there trying to stop it. She thought Travers was here, taking calls, but I've found him kind of tied up with other things. He thought Stephanie would take care of the desk, and vice versa. An unfortunate accident, that neither one was here to do so."

"Where is Travers now?" Judge Willis snapped, obviously not satisfied with the answer he'd received.

"In the holding area, tied up with the others,"

"Fine. When he is finished untying himself, I want him to call me. Is that clear, Stephen?" He ordered.

"Yes, sir. Very clear."

"Now, get back here. The connection was severed."

Drewer replaced the receiver and looked at Stephanie.

"You sneaky little..." she began to say.

"I didn't lie. You did find the toilet stuffed with paper, and Travers IS tied up."

They both joined in, interrupted by the radio. nodded. hearty laugh, before they were Stephanie hesitated. Drewer nodded.

"ONE this unit ELEVEN, acknowledge, please," the voice repeated.

Stephanie keyed the microphone and prepared herself for the questions that were about to be asked. "ELEVEN, this is ONE, go ahead."

There was a long, unbearable pause before the voice spoke again. "ONE, this is ELEVEN. We have some questions regarding the current situation here. Please be advised that we will be calling on the non-emergency line to discuss things. Acknowledge, over."

"Acknowledged." Stephanie said. She set the mike down and turned to Drewer. "Now what?" she asked, beginning to feel uneasy. "What am I gonna tell them?"

"Just remember," Drewer advised, "Whatever you tell them, don't lie."

"Oh," she replied. "I suppose I could twist things a bit, though, right?"

"You got it," he answered.

Chapter 9

MAKING THE BREAK

"State Police, can I help you?" Stephanie answered, lighting a cigarette. She'd sent Jack off to comb the offices for a pack before the phone rang. It had been nearly ten minutes since they said they'd call, which had made Stephanie a borderline nutcase.

"This is Sergeant Peterson, Troop C," he began. Stephanie realized then that the staged robbery must've been a terrific success if it had managed to require the assistance of Troop C as well as hers, Troop D.

"How may I help you, Sergeant?" Stephanie asked.

"I have been informed by an officer from your own barracks that you sounded like the dispatcher that had been booked an hour ago for assaulting an officer," he explained. "I would like to know if you, in fact, are Miss Stephanie Wilson, and if so, why you are NOT in jail."

Stephanie paused to choose one of the half-dozen explanations she'd memorized during the ten-minute wait. She opted for the one that sounded the least likely to be believed.

"Sir, I am Miss Wilson, and you are right. I am supposed to be in jail, but Lieutenant Travers was tied up, and the officer manning the desk is currently trying to stop the bathroom toilet from overflowing. To be blunt, sir, they were up the creek without a paddle, and I was the only other person around who knew how to handle the job."

There was a brief pause while the sergeant thought about her answer. Stephanie ground out her cigarette and lit another.

"Very well, Miss Wilson. I do not need to tell you the consequences should you decide to try and leave the building."

"No sir, you don't," she confirmed, smiling.

"Having said that," he continued, "we have a real problem on our hands at the liquor store on North Main Street. The person inside is refusing to negotiate for the moment, so we are stuck here."

Stephanie squelched the urge to stand up and cheer.

"What is it I can do to help, sir?" she asked instead.

"Inform Lieutenant Travers of the situation, and once that is done, please ask him to radio us with his recommendations. We are waiting for the sheriff to get here and don't wish to take action on our own."

"I'll do that, sir, immediately," she said. "Anything else?"

"No, man, that's all." Thank you. He hung up.

Stephanie sighed heavily as she returned the receiver to its cradle. "Oh God, that was close, she said to Drewer. "Now I have to tell Travers and..." She looked over her shoulder to find Drewer gone. She got up and went to the doorway. "Jack! Where are you?" she called out.

"Right here," he called from the direction of the bathroom. Seconds later he was at the end of the hall. "What's up?"

"Have you seen Drewer?" she asked.

"Right, here," Drewer answered as he reappeared behind Jack. "I went and told Travers for you about the liquor store."

"How did you know?" she inquired.

"I was on another line. I need to know every step, Laken, here. Everything is said."

"Why?" Jack challenged, turning on him. "So you can have us arrested, too? Who's to say you're not gonna take that box and all this information and use it against us?"

Drewer rolled his eyes. "Look," he replied, sounding irritated. "I am NOT going to use this information as evidence or anything like that. I just need to know; I can explain it to my uncle."

"Judge Willis?" Stephanie asked, growing hysterical.

"Why? He doesn't need to know."

"Oh yes, he does," Drewer insisted. "And I can assure you of two things, right now, that will happen when I fill him in."

"What's that?" Stephanie asked.

"First, he'll be tickled that this situation has been taken care of. We've been poring over the books to find a way out of this disaster Travers created, and now, it has taken care of itself. With little help, that is."

Stephanie noted that Drewer did look sincere, so that eased her mind a bit. "What's the second thing?" she queried.

"Second thing is," Drewer said with a smile, "when he hears what happened to Travers and how the woman did it to him, he'll laugh his ass off."

They did, too. For a moment, they were able to forget the mess they still had to clean up. Including that that lay on the floor, outside the bathroom.

"What did Travers have to say?" Jack asked, when they'd all stopped laughing,

"I don't know," Drewer replied. "All we had to do was tell him, right? Now, tell them they will have to wait for the sheriff because Lt. Travers had no answer."

"Okay," Stephanie said, "but you'll have to make the radio call, Jack. I have to get the inmates out."

Jack grinned. "Consider it done," he said.

"I have to get back to the courthouse," Drewer announced.

"What do we do after we get out of here?" Stephanie asked.

"Well, if there's no evidence and Trevor Doyle doesn't file charges against Elsie, nothing should happen. Take the folks home, and wait. I'll see to it that charges against you are dropped. You can convince. Willie of anything after this stunt. I'll take care of the minor stuff."

"And Travers?" Jack asked. "What about him?"

"I'll have a talk with him, Drewer promised". He will see that pursuing this matter could get ugly. He violated some procedures, and I can twist that around to sound like he'll be dropped down to patrolman again."

"I can add some threats to that as well. Don't worry."

He wandered past Stephanie towards the front door. They watched him as he paused before going through it.

"Mins Wilson," he said, turning to address her.

"Yeah?"

"I shouldn't say this, but I commend you for your courage. Nice job. I don't think I could've done it."

Stephanie smiled. "Thank you, sir."

"From now on, it's just Stephen, ok?"

She nodded. "And it's Stephanie."

He turned and left. Stephanie spun around and began to half-run towards the holding area.

"Stephanie," Jack called just as she was reaching for the doorknob. She turned to him and waited for what he had to say.

"I just wanted to say thanks," Jack said, uncomfortably. "I know it wasn't easy asking for my help. I am honored that you trusted me. enough to ask."

Stephanie was shocked. After being married to a person for 6 years, you can tell when they're lying. Jack wasn't. In fact, his ears were beet-red, which meant one thing: he was sincere and very, very embarrassed. Stephanie had not seen that side of him in three years or so. She couldn't quite recall when it was either.

"You always were there to help, Jack," she offered. "And regardless of what it may look like or sound like at times, I don't hate you."

She went through the door before he could say anything else. Now. Versation not the time for that sort of conversation.

Chapter 10

CLOSED QUARTERS & OPEN MOUTHS

The rain was coming down harder now, making it impossible to see the road. The driver of the news truck was having a very hard time seeing where he was going, and to make matters worse, he had nearly two dozen passengers packed in the truck like sardines.

And every last one of them was complaining or predicting disaster. Cheryl Martin, the news anchor from Channel Twelve, was somewhere in the back listening to Stephanie relate the day's events. Abandoning her front seat to do so, it had been filled instead by Jake Warner, who had not stopped talking since he'd got into the truck nearly forty minutes ago.

Jerry Richards, driver and cameraman, was ready to stop the truck and dump Warner on the side of the road.

The departure from the police station had been uninterrupted and easy. The appearance of the news truck in the town was not questioned because of the events going on at the liquor store. They'd chosen to drive in the direction of the "robbery," then take the detour around and out of town. Someone seeing it could later say that it was "there at the scene" but left, giving the appearance that its occupants had covered the story and then merely left. The liquor store was a big one—about the size of a grocery store—so the police did have their job cut out for them. Not one had even given the truck a second glance.

The rain had begun to fall as they were leaving. the station, though, at that time, it was just a gentle shower. Five miles or so outside of town, the gentle shower turned into a torrential downpour. The winds were gusting up to around 40 mph, and they were driving into that wind. Or trying to, anyway.

"...haven't seen it rain like this in years," Jake was saying, "You sure I can't smoke my pipe?"

Jerry Richards was using every ounce of energy he had, trying to control his temper, but this time he couldn't stop himself. "No!" he yelled, loudly enough so that everyone in the truck fell silent. "No! No! No! No! No! You have asked me that every ten minutes, and every time the answer is no, and it's no this time, and it'll be no for the whole damn ride!"

Jake simply looked at him and replied, "A simple yes or no was all I needed."

Jerry stomped on the brakes, bringing the truck to a stop. He put it in park and turned to Jake.

"Jerry!" Cheryl called from the back, "Why did we stop? Something wrong?"

He glared at Warner. "Yeah!" he answered. "I want you up here!"

"Why?" she yelled. "What's the problem?"

"I didn't know we had one," Jake protested, feeling like he'd been left out somehow. "Somethin' wrong with the truck? I know about trucks; I have one. Had one, in fact, for years. It's a..."

"I don't care," Richards snapped.

"What?" Jake asked, surprised.

"I said, I don't care, Mister Warner. There isn't anything wrong with this vehicle, either. The problem, sir, is you."

"Jerry, damnit!" Cheryl screeched from the rear, "What do you want? Answer me!"

"I'm the problem?" Jake said, pointing to himself with his right thumb. "How do you figure that? What did I do? " Jake turned in his seat so as to face Jerry, who ignored his co-worker and the stares of the others seated nearby. Among them was Elsie, and she could see the confrontation, but she couldn't quite hear over the sounds of the wind and rain. She leaned forward in her seat to see if she might hear a little better. George and Miriam were seated across from Elsie. Large trunk, containing some of the camera equipment. They exchanged worried looks, doing the same as Elsie: leaning forward to hear what was being said.

"You're the problem, because you won't stop flappin' your jaws," Jerry tried to explain, as calmly as he could. "You haven't shut up since we left the police station!"

"I have to," Jake protested. "And I can talk if I want to, as much as I want to!" "Not unless you want to walk home," Jerry threatened.

"Is that some kind of threat?" Warner inquired, his eyes narrowing to meet Richard's stare.

"It ain't any threat, Mister," Jerry replied. "If you don't keep yer mouth shut for the rest of the ride, the minute you open it. I'll dump you off on the side of the road. And if you open it to ask me about your pipe. and smokin' it. I won't stop. I'll just lean over, open that door, and push you out!"

"You can't do that!" Warner yelled.

He wasn't aware of what had happened the last time He yelled those very same words.

Stephanie was seated on the floor, at the very back of the truck. Seated next to her was Cheryl Martin, the woman who had engineered this escape and the diversion that had made their departure so easy. Both of them were squeezed into the corner near the doors, and without any interior lights on, seeing anything was impossible. They fought to stand up, and finally doing so, helped each other begin the treacherous journey forward.

Elsie leaped out of her seat and lunged at Jerry, wrapping her left arm around his chest from behind. She used her right to grab hold of his hair, which she began to pull as hard as she could. She had moved so quickly that neither George nor Miriam had a chance to stop her. It was so dark that all they'd seen was a shadow, and when Richards began to yell. George knew that Shadow was responsible.

It reappeared again, and he grabbed at it, pulling the shadow's arm towards him. He ignored the scream and knocked the person over onto the floor, taking his horrified wife with him. She had tried to stop him from falling but failed.

Jerry had stopped the truck right in the road. He hadn't pulled it off to the side, nor had he put his directional light on. The motor was running, the headlights were on, and there it sat—on a long stretch of road without streetlights—the interior lit only by the lights from the dashboard.

Jake couldn't see anything or anybody, except his spouse. He sat in his seat, frozen in place by the sight of his wife attacking Richards. (Still wearing that awful dress with the clashing apron). He had no idea why she was doing it, either.

The sounds of cursing and screaming, as well as objects crashing around in the back, added to his confusion. The truck was actually beginning to shake with all the moving around inside. Jake didn't move. For some reason his wife was trying to kill the driver, and there was a brawl in the back, but he just couldn't move.

Instead, he winced as something crashed to the floor in the back, and Richard yelled a little louder.

"They're late. Stephen." Judge Willis stated.

"You said one hour, and they're late."

Drewer looked at his watch again.

"I said one hour, that's true," he confirmed, "but I didn't say they'd be here in an hour."

"What?" Willis asked, "What are you talkin' about?" Didn't you tell me they'd be leaving the station in an hour?"

"Yes, sir."

"Then where are they?" Willis demanded, rising from his chair slowly.

Drewer glanced at his watch and did some quick figuring in his head.

"If they left on time and didn't run into any problems," Stephen answered, "I'd say they're just about fifteen miles outside of town."

Judge Willis's face went sheet-white, and his jaw dropped open in shock.

Drewer leaned back in his chair and smiled.

Chapter 11

HOMEWARD BOUND

Lt. Travers focused on the leg of the bench in the opposite cell and ignored the efforts of those around him to get his attention.

He blinked at the flash of light and winced when it flashed again.

"Alright, alright, that's sufficient," Willis said. "Now, would someone do the honors of untying Mister Travers, please?" One of the officers stepped forward, stifling his snickering, and began to untie Travers' ankles.

"I hope I've made myself clear, Mister Travers," Drewer said. "It will be better if you just leave things alone."

Travers used his freed hands to pull Elsie's undies from his mouth, which he threw to the floor in anger.

"Drewer," he answered, "I don't give a damn what you threaten me with. They broke out of jail and assaulted me. I have a right and responsibility to do something about it."

Drewer and Willis exchanged glances.

"You'll make things worse." Drewer argued. "Things have worked out here. Why can't you leave it alone?"

"You seem to think this is all so very, very funny, don't you, Drewer?" Travers snapped, rising stiffly from the chair he'd been tied into. "You have broken the lav and then come here to mock me by taking pictures!"

He reached out and yanked the camera, but Drewer anticipated the move. The tug-o-war was over quickly.

"Judge Willis and I are leaving," Drewer announced. "You do whatever you want, but you have been warned and will not be offered any further immunity in the future. You will be held accountable for your actions. Got it?"

"I got it," Travers snapped. "Now. If you don't mind, I have a job to do."

He walked stiffly out of the cell to the door, ignoring the chuckles from the officers gathered in the holding area. "Everyone in the briefing room, now!" he bellowed and disappeared through the door.

Drewer bent over and retrieved Elsie's undies.

"Souvenir," he said simply, grinning at his uncle.

They both laughed, each wondering where the bunch from Knicker's Notch was now and what could possibly happen next.

Megan Doyle sat, stunned, staring at the white wall of her hospital room. Upon it flashed scenes from the last twelve hours, though none contained the events just told to her. Hard as she tried to imagine it. She could not quite envision Elsie Warner shooting her husband in the ass.

"Mrs. Doyle?" the voice called, bringing her back to the present conversation.

"Huh? Oh, yeah. I'm sorry," she apologized.

"That's alright, Ma'am," the trooper said, smiling.

"You needn't worry, though. Your husband will be fine, and you can see him soon. And, hey, your two young sons are just fine, too, so..."

"Where's Elsie Warner?" she suddenly asked.

"Well," he replied, caught off guard, "she was in jail."

"Was?"

"Yes, Ma'am," he confirmed, beginning to fidget with his hat in his hands.

He contemplated his answer before going on.

"We had to arrest just about everyone at the scene," he explained, "and then they all, uh...broke out."

Megan's jaw dropped again, for the second time in the conversation, "BROKE OUT?" she was finally able to say. "You mean they ESCAPED?"

The trooper winced at the sound of the last word, a sore spot for all involved.

"Yes, Ma'am," he answered, "but we're out looking for them now, and rest assured, we're gonna find them."

State Trooper Karen Jordan had done just that. She'd passed the stationary Channel 12 news truck going southbound and noted it wasn't moving. The fact it was sitting in the road and not even pulled to the side alarmed her, so she turned her cruiser around and returned to investigate.

She hated having to leave the dry confines of her cruiser, but there was really no other way to check on the occupants of the truck. She put the cruiser in park, firmly planted her hat on her head, and fought the wind to open her door. It never crossed her mind to radio in her intentions, as she wasn't expecting any trouble.

Cheryl Martin was a friend of hers. A good one, too, whom she'd just about grown up with—with the exception of the two years Cheryl had spent at the University of Maine.

Although it was rare that their schedules cooperated, they still got together often enough to be seen as the best of friends.

Karen allowed the wind to slam her door and began the uncomfortable walk up the driver's side of the truck. She'd taken only half a dozen steps when she turned around, quite abruptly.

"He's changed his mind," Jake Warner announced, "See, I told ya' they hate this weather."

Warner's interpretation of what Stephanie saw in the driver's-side mirror was absurd, and she knew it. Rather than explain otherwise—risking another brawl—she chose to ignore him. "I think I know what he's doing," she said.

Sure enough, the trooper returned to the cruiser to activate the blue lights—a precautionary measure.

Everyone in the truck seemed to gasp in horror.

"We've been caught," Elsie called from behind Stephanie.

"Else," Jake replied, trying to sound patient with his spouse, "PLEASE just keep it sealed."

"Sealed?" she snapped, "What sealed?"

"Yer mouth, he shot back, "what else?"

"Well, don't you have a lot of nerve?" she said, angrily. "You just caused the biggest brawl in history because you wouldn't shut yer' mouth, and NOW, you're tellin' ME to keep my mouth 'sealed'? HOW DARE YOU!"

"Someone should'a stuffed those panties of hers' in HER mouth instead of the cop's," Jerry muttered, though he intended to be heard.

"Listen, you camera-totin' little..." Warner began, coming to the defense of his wife.

"For God's sake, STOP!" Stephanie shrieked, turning to face the shadows behind her. "ALL OF YOU SHUT UP! You're acting like a bunch of kids on a school bus! If this guy hears you, you will get caught!"

"Who put you in charge?" Warner shot back.

"Who got you out of jail?" she snapped, turning to face his silhouette.

Warner didn't respond. "Well, well, well," Richards said slowly and sarcastically, "Mister diarrhea-mouth finally runs out of liquid."

"Here he comes," Stephanie announced, but no one was listening.

The truck commenced to shake again with the movement inside.

Karen Jordan had decided it best to put the blue lights on, considering the inclement weather. The visibility was very poor, and anyone could easily come up and slam into her cruiser as well as the truck.

Approaching the driver's side window, she noticed the unusual sounds coming from within. She couldn't quite tell what, exactly, they were, but they were strange and loud. Loud enough to be heard over the wind and rain.

Karen shined her flashlight upwards into the window of the truck and noted two more strange things: the window was steamed up—almost to the point of making it impossible to see inside—and secondly, there appeared to be no one in the driver's seat.

She fought to hold the hat on her head, as the wind seemed to pick up, and stood on her toes to peer inside.

She heard the scream quite clearly, and that was enough for her.

Stephanie was sitting on Jerry's lower legs, trying to help George Mitchell hold him down. Jake Warner was using every ounce of energy he had to get at him. They were wedged in a pig pile, between the driver's seat and passenger's, and Cheryl Martin was fighting to get Elsie off her back. In the darkness, Elsie couldn't see anything (and apparently didn't care), as Cheryl had tried to help in holding back Jake. Elsie didn't take too kindly to anybody touching her husband for any reason (a point already made in previous altercations). She grabbed Cheryl and jumped on her back while grabbing a fistful of her hair.

It was Cheryl who had screamed.

Trooper Karen Jordan, however, was fueled by the sound of the scream itself. She knew it was a woman, and because she knew who drove this truck, she was relatively sure she knew who that scream belonged to.

Her best friend, and that added desperation to her emotions of anger and confusion over this strange scene.

She tried to open the driver's side door, but it was locked. So, she ran around the front end to the passenger side. It was locked, too.

"Back here!" a voice called, to her left. Karen squinted in the lights shining from her cruiser, seeing a profile near the back of the truck, waving.

She bolted for the person beckoning her, losing her hat to the wind as she did so. She didn't recognize the woman whose face came into view as she slid to a halt on the pavement.

"Do something, PLEASE!" Marge Burroughs pleaded.

"They'll kill each other if you don't!"

Karen noted the nasty scratch marks—apparently made by someone's fingernails—on the right side of Marge's face.

"Who?" Karen yelled over the wind and driving rain.

"Who's gonna kill who?"

"I dunno!" Marge screamed, stomping angrily. "They're all fighting, and ya can't see an inch in front of yer' own face!"

"I'll have to call for help!" Karen yelled. "I can't do this myself!"

"NO! NO!" Marge shrieked. "You can't!" The idea of it horrified Marge, knowing they'd all be back in jail.

"Why not?" Karen asked.

"No time to explain," she responded. "Just do what you can to stop 'em, please?"

Against her better judgment and training, Karen did. She turned and leaped in the back door and cast her flashlight beam down the length of the truck's interior. She couldn't see much, but what she did see, she could not believe.

Chapter 12

BEST FRIEND AND BRIBERY

Jake reached in the breast pocket of his overalls and removed his red and white bandana. He gave his nose a "honk" and then dabbed at the perspiration on his forehead. Elsie was seated on the same storage trunk, to Jake's left. She straightened her dress and folded the two pieces of cloth that had once been her apron. Someone had ripped it off her, trying to pull her off of Cheryl. She noticed several strands of hair tangled in her wedding rings and began pulling them out.

George and Marlene were seated on the floor next to Marge Burroughs, who continued to question aloud who it was who'd scratched her.

Jerry Richards was back in the driver's seat, rubbing the spot on his head where Elsie had been yanking his hair. Cheryl was doing the same, although she was also muttering obscenities as she did so.

Everyone was seated—either on a makeshift seat or on the floor—trying to regain their senses. Trooper Karen Jordan was standing midway down the length of the truck, waiting for someone to answer her questions. Even her best friend refused to offer any explanations. She'd gotten Jerry to pull the truck off to the side of the road, but that was all the cooperation she had received.

"Look, everybody," Karen warned, "If I don't get an explanation, I'm gonna take all of you in. Do you understand me? ALL of you."

"Oh terrific," Stephanie muttered behind her. "Another Travers."

"What was that?" Karen asked, turning around.

"I said, TERRIFIC," Stephanie repeated.

"I heard that part," Karen said, "But repeat the name you used."

"Travers." Stephanie squirmed and resisted the urge to spit after saying it.

"Lieutenant Travers?" Karen questioned.

"Yes," Stephanie snapped, growing tired of the line of questions. "The one and only."

Karen held Stephanie's gaze for a moment, then scanned the faces around her. The interior lights were now on but provided little light. Most met her stare for a few seconds, while others refused to look at her.

Karen spun around to face her best friend, with a horrified look on her face. "OH MY GOD, CHERYL!" she shrieked. "THESE ARE THE PEOPLE THAT..."

Cheryl leaned back in her seat and just smiled.

"That's right," she said. "The very same ones."

"WHAT ARE YOU DOING?" Karen screamed in disbelief.

"Do you have ANY idea the trouble you're in, here?" I mean, have you lost your mind or what?"

Cheryl rose from her seat and looked around the truck. "I knew it," she said flatly. "I knew it, know it now, and have no intentions of changing my mind."

"But Cheryl," Karen pleaded, "this is nuts!"

"Karen, calm yourself," Cheryl ordered. "You can't talk me out of it, so don't try. I admit, I didn't anticipate the riot that just occurred, and I'll probably lose my job when the boss sees the damage these convicts have done." She paused to smile at the faces staring back at her. "I don't know what sort of warped version of the story you heard, Karen, but whatever it was, it isn't true. I wanted the truth and firmly believe that what I've learned IS just that. THE TRUTH. It IS my job to report it, remember?"

Karen simply stared back at her.

"Well, isn't it?" Cheryl prodded.

"Yes," Karen muttered quietly, reluctantly surrendering to her friend's insanity. "Fine, it's your job and all that," she confirmed, "but it's NOT your job to aid in a jail break. It is NOT your job to provide transportation to those you ILLEGALLY break out of jail. It is NOT your responsibility to oversee them, regardless of what you believe or not. IT IS MY JOB, HOWEVER, TO ENFORCE THE LAW, AND YOU'RE BREAKING IT, CHERYL. IN A VERY BIG WAY."

"Yes, I am, Karen. So, get off your soapbox and either arrest me or shut up."

Karen felt her ears turn red. It was an instant physical sign that she was angry. She was trying to deal with this situation objectively, considering her closest friend was involved.

She turned and scanned the faces once again. "Which one of you is the woman who shot the police officer?"

Elsie slowly raised her hand.

"Was it an accident?" Karen inquired.

"Yes, Ma'am," Elsie acknowledged.

Karen could see the shame in her expression, and with that, she turned back to face Cheryl. She closed her eyes, sighed, then reopened them. "Where are you headed?"

"Knicker's Notch," Cheryl replied, grinning.

"I'm not sure that's such a good idea," Karen offered, running her fingers through her drenched hair.

She realized, then, her hat was gone. "That will be the first place they look for you. I guarantee it."

"Who did YOU think it was when you saw the truck?"

Cheryl asked.

"You...but," Karen replied.

"But, what?" Cheryl interrupted. "You thought it was just the news truck with Jerry and me. They'll think the same thing. Our reason for going into Knicker's Notch is to cover this story."

"Cheryl," Karen said, rolling her eyes, "Don't you think they'll want to search this truck?"

"She's got a point, there," Jake Warner spoke up.

"They may know you and all that, but they'll want to take a look inside just as a precaution."

Karen nodded emphatically. "They will, Cheryl. Count on it."

"Well, they won't look inside if you're escorting us, now, will they?" Cheryl asked.

"Oh, now, wait a minute, Cheryl," Karen began, "HOW can you expect me to do that? Do you realize what you're asking me to do? You're asking ME to break the law!"

"So."

"Whadd'ya mean, so?" Karen half-yelled, throwing up her arms in anger.

"You've already broken it," Cheryl reminded her, "by not reporting that you've found us."

"I still could, if I wanted to," Karen snapped, feeling her ears turning red again.

"You could," Cheryl agreed, "but you won't."

"What makes you so sure?"

Cheryl grinned and chose her words carefully. She wanted to make her point, but not in such a way that Karen would be embarrassed.

"You owe me one, Cheryl reminded her.

"Since when and for what?" Karen challenged, placing her hands on her hips.

"Two-thirty a.m., February eleventh, nineteen eighty-four," Cheryl stated, as if reading from a UPI wire snippet.

Karen searched her memory but failed to recall the significance of the date and time. Cheryl saw the confused look and added, "Does the year mean anything?"

"We graduated that year," Karen answered, "but what..." Her jaw dropped.

"If I look hard enough," Cheryl said, "I think I might just find those choice pictures."

Karen had gotten very drunk and gone for a run down the street to the convenience store. The problem was, she was barefoot and only wearing a pillowcase, which she'd cut holes in to wear as a shirt. (She'd chosen one with a floral design.) The pillowcase didn't quite cover everything...in fact, it only came down to the bottom of her hips. Cheryl had, as an up-and-coming journalist, been compelled to take a few rear-view shots (no pun intended) before she chased Karen down to bring her home.

"You wouldn't dare," Karen challenged, the blood draining from her face..

"I would."

"But, why?" Karen asked, "How can you do this to me?"

"WHY are you doing it?"

"Do you trust me, Karen?"

She nodded. "Completely."

"Then trust me on this, please," Cheryl pleaded.

"Do you really believe in them that much?"

This time it was Cheryl who replied, "Completely."

Karen closed her eyes and weighed the arguments at hand.

"Alright," she finally surrendered. "If I do this, I have a few conditions, Cheryl."

"Name 'em, dearie."

"First," she began, holding up one finger, "You all will do EXACTLY AS I TELL YOU. Two, I will ride ahead of the truck, and should we meet up with some of my co-workers, I will tell them to let you through. I WILL NOT say I checked the truck, so if they insist and catch you, my butt won't be in a sling. Does everyone understand this so far"?

There were "yes" and grunts of acknowledgment all around.

"Third," Karen continued, "YOU WILL ALL BEHAVE. NO MORE BRAWLS. You should be sticking together, not trying to dismember each other. So, NO MORE FIGHTS.

Got that, Mister Warner? Mrs. Warner?"

Jake and Elsie nodded but wouldn't meet her stare. Instead, they focused on their feet.

"Jerry?" Karen asked. "You got that?"

He nodded.

"Good, now one more thing, Cheryl."

"What's that, Officer Jordan?" She replied, smiling triumphantly.

"Prior to nine a.m. on Monday morning," Karen said, "You WILL find those choice photos and negatives, and you WILL surrender them to me."

Chapter 13

UNAUTHORIZED ENTRY

"Damnit," George Mitchell cursed, tripping over something in the dark and nearly falling.

"Watch yer self, George," Jake warned from behind him.

"Thanks for the warning, Jake," he grumbled, fumbling for something to hold onto. He needed to steady himself before going on. "Are you sure you know where the switches are?"

"For Pete's sake," Jake snapped, irritably, "I've been livin' on this rock for 40 years and been in this store every day. Of course, I know where the light switches are!"

George and Jake were making their way to the back of Warren's store. It was pitch black, and with the exception of the occasional flash of lightning outside, they had only their eyes and sense of direction to rely on.

The truck, preceded by Karen Jordan's cruiser, had made the trip up the mountain without a problem. They saw no one. They passed no one. The storm—as nasty as it was—had been a stroke of much-needed luck. It kept everyone else off the roads. Marlene had suggested they stop at the store first, as it seemed a sensible place for them all to convene. It had a small counter, and they could all settle in for some coffee while they discussed their next move.

George and Jake had volunteered to venture inside. and find the lights. They had to pry open the front door with a crowbar first, as Warren wasn't around to open up.

"Are you men alright?" Karen Jordan called from the doorway.

"Just fine," George grumbled, daring to take two more steps.

"I am sorry 'bout not having my flashlight," she apologized. "I had it when I got in the news truck, but Lord knows what happened to it..."

"She's probably holding it and doesn't know it." Jake muttered. "Women bein' police officers..."

"I'm sure she's a fine police officer, George argued, unsure if he believed it himself. "She just lost it, is all."

"Yup" was all Jake would say.

"Hey, Warren, there's lights on in the store." Burroughs called from the living room.

A second or two later, Warren rounded the corner with Coleman lantern lighting his way. A birthday gift that year, he was finally getting to use. "Burr, there can't be any lights on, he said wearily. "The power is out, remember?"

"Well, Warren, if ya' don't believe me, see for yourself," Burroughs replied, stepping aside from the window that looked towards the tiny square.

Warren changed places with him, handing him the lantern. He pulled back the curtain and peered out. "Son-of-a-gun," he muttered, "you're right. There are lights on. They're movin' around, though, so they must have flashlights."

"Who could it be, Warren?" Burroughs whispered, as if the store's intruders would hear him.

"Well, it ain't Marlene or anyone else we know," he concluded. "Last we knew, they were in jail."

"Which means what?" Burroughs asked.

"Which means that whoever's in there, ain't s'posed to be," Warren explained angrily. "They broke in."

Warren observed the goings-on for another minute or so before turning around and taking his lantern back. He had to do something, or the thieves would steal him blind.

"Maybe we ought to call the cops," Burroughs suggested, unaware how ludicrous a suggestion that was.

"Burr," Warren said slowly, "what happened the last time the police were called?"

Burroughs thought about that for a moment.

"Right. We call the police, and they'll mess this up somehow," Warren continued. "So let's you and me grab a shotgun and go have ourselves a look."

Burroughs didn't like that idea at all, but it sure beat calling the police, so he nodded and gestured for his friend to lead the way.

After delivering twins on the floor of that store earlier that day, going after a couple of thieves seemed like a breeze. His ears were still ringing from listening to Megan scream.

"I wish to heck the light switch was as easy to find as these flashlights," George said, shining his up and down the wall to his right.

"I'm just glad ya' found 'em," Jake replied, using his to examine the left one. "It was getting' a bit too hazardous fumbling around here in the dark."

"I thought you knew where the switch was," George snapped.

"I thought it was out back, near the sink," Jake explained. "Warren must've moved it or somethin'g."

"Yeah, sure," George responded, sarcastically. "He rewired the store just like he re-did the plumbing."

"He did?" Jake asked, astonished. "Gee, I didn't know that. Warren's really talented, then, huh'?" George couldn't believe that Jake was that naive.

"Yeah," he agreed, rather than argue the point, "just keep looking."

"Is this thing loaded?" Burroughs asked, following Warren across the field.

"Of course, it's loaded," Warren snapped. "Why in hell wouldn't it be?"

"I dunno," Burroughs observed, "I just don't..."

"Burr, for Pete's sake, shut yer' mouth," Warren interrupted. "We don't want to be heard!"

They were approaching the store diagonally, headed for the front door, across an open field that lay between it and Warren's house. It was still pouring, and they'd left behind the lantern, taking a small flashlight instead. The field was small, though, and in the dark, just as treacherous.

"Hey! George! I found it!" Jake called out, scaring him half to death.

George spun around and knocked some cans off the shelf beside him with his arm. "Jees!" he cried out, "Did ya' have to yell like that?"

"Sorry, George," Jake apologized. "Just glad I found it, that's all."

"Yeah, well, just turn 'em on." George snapped.

"I gotta pick up the mess I just made."

"Oh hell," Warren cursed, "Did ya' hear that? They're trashing my store!"

"Well, what are you going to do about it, Warren?" Burroughs asked, crouched beside him, next to the porch.

"I'm gonna make 'em pick it up, for starters," he threatened, pumping a round into his shotgun. Warren stood up and began to climb the stairs that led to the front door. Burroughs watched in horror, unable to move. Warren mumbled something, then turned to find Burroughs still hiding beside the porch. He waved at him frantically, trying to get him to join him. Burroughs only moved when there was such a loud crack of thunder; he was scared into doing so.

"What's the matter?" Warren snapped, kneeling just below the windows.

"I'm scared, Warren," admitted Burroughs, kneeling down next to him. "I have never done this before."

"Well, neither have I," Warren whispered, "but they don't know that, right?" He gestured to the thieves inside the store. "They aren't gonna argue with two shotguns pointed at their privates now, are they?"

Burroughs only gasped at the thought and watched Warren rise to enter the store.

"Damnit," Jake cursed, trying the switch several times to be sure.

"Power must be out," George observed. "Doesn't surprise me, though. This is the worst storm we've had in years."

"Better go out back and let 'em know," Jake said.

"See if you can get a lantern or some more flashlights, George replied, and tell them there won't be any coffee here tonight."

Jake and George shared a chuckle and began to turn in opposite directions. George pointed his flashlight towards the back door, forgetting about the cans he'd knocked over. One step was all it took, and down he went, screaming and swearing. Warren came through the front door then, doing exactly the same.

"Alright, don't anybody move!" Warren yelled.

"I'll blow ya ta' hell and back!"

"Me, too!" Burroughs added, pointing his shotgun at the figure on the floor.

"Warren!" Jake hollered, hands up above his head.

"Jake? That you?" Warren asked, shining his flashlight in Jake's face.

"Yeah," he answered, putting his hand in front of his face to shield his eyes, "You scared us to death!"

"What in hell are you doin' here?" Warren asked.

"We thought you were in jail."

"Long story," Jake replied. "Wanna stop shinin' that in my face?"

"Oh, sorry," Warren said, turning towards the figure lying on the floor. "Is that you, George? You alright?"

"Just wonderful," he muttered, rolling over. "I think my back is busted, though."

Burroughs set his shotgun down and went to help George off the floor.

"Jake," Warren said, leaning his gun against the counter, "might I ask what you were doin', breakin' into my store?"

"We broke in, cause you weren't around to let us in," Jake replied.

"What did you want?"

"Coffee," Jake answered, smiling. "And some pipe tobacco, too."

"That doesn't make it right," Warren protested.

"You BROKE IN, Jake."

"I guess you could say we had the approval of the police department," Jake explained.

"I doubt that, Jake." Warren argued.

"If you don't believe me, Jake insisted, "just go out back and talk to that lady state police officer. She watched us do it."

Warren just stared at Jake in disbelief.

"I told you, Warren, it's a long story," Jake added. "So, sit down for a minute, and I'll fill ya' in.

"No, thanks." Warren replied, "I'll stand for this."

"Suit yer'self, Jake said.

Chapter 14

THE CHASE IS ON

"Consider yourself suspended without pay," Travers snapped, "and that's indefinitely, Mister Wilson."

"Well, sir," Jack replied, "that's the first I've heard of an officer being suspended for plunging a toilet. I'll just have to practice while on suspension."

"It's not for that, and you know it. Mister!" Travers yelled back, rising from his chair to point his right finger at Jack. "And don't you use that tone of voice with me! You know why you're being suspended!"

Jack resisted the urge to smile. He knew he was rattling Travers' cage and knew, too, that his refusing to help infuriated him more. Still, he didn't care.

"I told you, sir," Jack replied calmly, "I don't know anything. That's the truth."

"Get out of here, Jack," Travers ordered, "before you end up fired. Just get out of my office!"

Jack turned and left without another word.

Travers sat back down and tried to collect his thoughts. He was absolutely enraged that the Knicker's Notch Gang had not yet been found. He had an All Points Bulletin out on them, and every state police officer was out searching, but nothing had turned up. No one had seen them leave, and no one had found out how, either. Lt. Traver was being made the butt of all kinds of jokes, and he didn't like it. Not one bit. The harder he tried, however, to get to the bottom of the matter, the more difficult things became. There were no answers. There were no clues. There were no witnesses. And no evidence, either. That particular aspect baffled him most. ALL of the evidence surrounding the shooting in Knicker's Notch had mysteriously disappeared. Every scrap of paper and every photo taken of the group. It was as if it had grown wings and flown.

"This whole investigation is going down the toilet," Travers remarked, to no one but himself.

It only took a few seconds for him to make the connection between the evidence and the backed-up toilet.

"JACK," he screamed, bounding over his desk. "GET BACK HERE!!!!"

Jack, of course, was long gone.

"I'm waiting for the punch line, Jake," Warren finally remarked.

"Punch line?" Jake asked, puffing on his pipe.

"Yeah," Warren said, "punch line. This is all a joke, right?"

"No, Warren," Jake answered, "it's not. It's the truth, though; I s'pose some of it had some laughs mixed in somewhere. Hell, we had to laugh, right?"

Burroughs chuckled a bit, then stifled it when Warren shot him a nasty look. "It's NOT funny," he told Burroughs. "Think about it, Burr. They're bein' chased by the ENTIRE State Police Force!"

"Not quite," Jake interjected.

"Huh?" Warren grunted, confused.

"Not quite," Jake repeated. "We have one lady cop outside who ain't chasing' us."

Warren rolled his eyes and shook his head.

Oh and their dispatcher too, he added with a smirk.

"Now what, Jake?" he asked.

Jake leaned back against the counter and re-lit his pipe, puffing a couple of times. "I don't really know, Warren."

"Well, well, well," Warren said, conclusively. "I don't believe I'm hearing' this. Jake Warner admitting he doesn't know something'. That's a first."

"Warren," Jake said, rather softly, "Elsie never shot anybody before. I know it was an accident, but try' to prove it. is a whole different problem altogether. I ain't no lawyer and I don't know the law."

Warren realized that Jake was doing more than admitting he didn't know everything. He was admitting he was scared, and that deserved a bit of respect. He decided to leave the smart remarks out of it.

"Well," Warren replied, "let's all go out and discuss this together. Whatever we do, we do together."

"Fair enough," Jake answered, shaking Warren's hand.

"Sorry 'bout the mess in here."

"We'll discuss THAT, when THIS is over, Warren said with a grin.

"Stephen, I've been thinking," Judge Willis mumbled. through a mouthful of steak and eggs. He chewed for a moment and sipped his coffee, collecting his thoughts as he did so.

They were seated in Willis' kitchen, enjoying an early morning breakfast, which Willis' wife had cooked. She had, at first, refused his request for her to get up "and cook somethin', I'm starvin'." She'd seen the time through squinted eyes and told him [in a not so nice way] to cook it himself. She changed her mind, quite rapidly, when he informed her that her favorite nephew was hungry, too. Breakfast having been served, she'd politely excused herself and gone back to bed. Three in the morning was not a good hour for her; she'd apologized.

Judge Willis cleared his throat and explained his line of thought. "If Lieutenant Travers has no witnesses or evidence to anything that has happened," he proposed, "then what, if anything, can he do?"

Stephen Drewer didn't hesitate for a second.

"Not a damn thing, sir," he said. "He can chase 'em down and arrest 'em all, but there's nothing to charge 'em with. He can't prove they escaped from jail, 'cause there's no evidence they were ever there. If Doyle doesn't press charges for Elsie Warner's minor infraction of the law, he paused to smile, then he can't arrest her, either."

"What about his being hog-tied up in jail?" Willis pressed, stuffing the last piece of steak in his mouth.

"It's his word against their's," Stephen answered. "We untied him, but no one actually SAW who tied him up."

Willis thought about that for a moment, sipping the last of his coffee. He wiped his mouth with a napkin, then leaned back, folding his arms across his chest.

"There's one piece of evidence, though," Willis observed. "Elsie's undies."

"And I have those," Stephen reminded him. "So there is no evidence. Physical or otherwise."

"So," Willis concluded, "if Travers goes after them and brings them in, he's gonna make a jackass out of himself."

"That's correct, sir," Stephen replied. "In a very big way."

"Are we gonna stop him?" Willis asked. "I mean, we should do something' to stop these poor people from going through any more. Even Jake Warner doesn't deserve to be dragged through the pigpen THAT much."

"No, he doesn't," Stephen agreed, finishing the last of his eggs. "But Lieutenant Travers DOES, and we should let the folks in Knicker's Notch do the draggin'g."

Judge Willis simply smiled.

"We'll just make sure," Stephen added, "that they don't find themselves rolling in it, themselves."

Enough said, thought Willis. He knew now that all he could do was wait for Travers' next move.

"Haven't you gotten me in enough trouble as it is?" Officer Karen Jordan asked irritably. "My God, Cheryl, I don't believe you."

"Just do this one more thing," she pleaded, "and that's it. I promise."

"You're lucky. I'm in uniform, and it's so damn dark in here," Karen snapped. They were standing in the bathroom at Jake and Elsie Warner's home, where the entire group had decided to move to for the time being.

"Why is that?" Cheryl asked.

"If I could see you and I wasn't on duty," Karen replied, "I'd slap you so hard those implants of yours' would wind up on the other side of you."

Cheryl half-shrieked at that remark, cringing at the thought simultaneously. "Come on, Karen," she pleaded, "it's not a big deal."

"Radioing in false information IS a big deal, Cheryl," she corrected her. "I can't warp the truth and get away with it like you do."

"You can just word it so it SOUNDS like the truth," Cheryl insisted. "It's raining so hard out there; you only need to advise them, right?"

Karen thought for a minute, unsure as to what she should do. Somehow, she already knew the decision had been made for her.

"Hello, Mike," greeted the deep, friendly voice on the other end of the line.

"Daniel, my good ol' friend," Travers greeted, glad to hear a pleasant voice. "What can I do for you?"

"Well," Sergeant Peterson said, "I think it's more like what I can do for you. I have some information you might be interested in."

"Oh yeah," Travers replied, picking up a pen and sifting through the pile on his desk for something to write on. "What's that?"

"It may be nothing," Peterson cautioned, "but it was enough to pique my curiosity, and I looked into it a bit. One of my officers who patrols the Knicker's Notch area called in 'bout an hour ago. She said that the water was so high at the foot of the mountain that Miner's Creek was gonna make that road impassable soon."

Traver scribbled furiously, his heart leaping as well as his curiosity at the mere mention of the Som Knicker's Notch. "Go on," he prodded, pausing to wait for the rest.

"Well," Peterson continued, "I made note of it and told the dispatcher to advise our units to steer clear for the time being. The only thing is, one of the men called in and said he'd JUST driven over the darn bridge and the water ain't high enough to close it."

Travers digested that information for a moment.

"So," he concluded, "what do you think is so strange?"

"It wouldn't be strange," Peterson replied, "if he ALSO hadn't been sitting just off the road and seen the channel 12 news truck pass by a couple hours earlier."

"And?" Travers questioned, missing the point.

"Unit twelve was leading the way, Peterson explained, "and I got to thinking about all this Knicker's Notch stuff. You had sixteen people escape, and you don't know HOW they got out of there, unseen, and ..."

"I'll be damned," Travers exclaimed, "they're in the news truck."

"Maybe," Peterson corrected.

"Danny, ol' boy," Travers said, excitedly, "I'll bet you dinner and a case of beer they are in that truck."

"You're on, Mike," Peterson agreed. "Now what?" Travers paused for a moment, then began letting his buddy in on his plans. The chase was on.

Chapter 15

CHASING SHADOWS

Living so far up a mountain and so many miles away from a town forces one to keep themselves prepared for all sorts of emergencies. The winter, for example, makes travel down the mountain impossible and often renders the acquisition of supplies impossible as well. It will often knock the power out, too, and unlike living in a town or big city, where it is often restored in a matter of hours, you might find yourself waiting days for that to happen.

As a result, in Knicker's Notch, everyone is prepared—so well, in fact, that they could rely on themselves for weeks on end. Warren's store is well-stocked (overstocked in winter months), and the residents themselves maintain a ready supply of food, water, and survival equipment in their homes. Basically, the items included in their homes are the same as what one would take on a camping trip, with various other things they consider necessities (soda, candy, etc.).

The storm's arrival at Knicker's Notch, therefore, simply didn't bother anyone. The power was out, but all that was needed were some lanterns and camping stoves.

Finding the lanterns was no problem—Jake had two, and five more were found in the others' darkened basements. The camping stoves, numbering three, were put to use as well. Jake raided his chicken coop for the eggs, and Warren scooped up bacon, bread, and various other items from the store to complete the breakfast menu.

Marge Burroughs, Elsie Warner, and Marlene Corbett volunteered to do the cooking, while many of the others grabbed blankets and attempted to sleep for a little while.

The rain was coming down so hard that Jake was surprised to see the roof leaking again. It had not done so since early spring, nearly twelve years before. That alone was an indication of the serious nature of the storm, and that convinced him and the others that no one would be anywhere nearby. No one would venture up the mountain in such awful weather. No sane person, anyway.

After shoving a bucket under the waterfall coming from the living room ceiling, Jake and the rest of the men sat down to play themselves a game of poker. The only one who chose not to play was George, whose back was too sore to sit upright. He had retired to the guest room and was checked periodically by Burroughs and, of course, Miriam, his wife.

Jake looked again at the cards in his hands, then glanced up and across the table at John Melbourne.

"What's wild, again?" Jake asked.

"I'm gonna be, if you ask that one more time," John snapped. "I told you before, jacks and jokers."

"Oh, yeah," Jake said, ignoring John's nasty tone. "Thanks for repeatin' yer'self."

"Go ahead. Mister Burroughs," John said, turning to him. "It's your bet."

"I'm foldin'," Burroughs announced, obviously disgusted with his cards. He tossed them in the center of the table and crossed his arms.

"Burr," Jake replied, "are you sure you know how to play this game? Hell, you haven't made a single bet yet."

"Of course, I know how to play," Burroughs shot back. "You know that. I can't help it if I don't get the cards I need."

Burroughs adopted the expression of a pouting four-year-old.

"Maybe we should play something else," Andy Pierce suggested, "like Rummy."

"No." Burroughs replied abruptly. "Poker is fine."

"Then stop acting' childish," said Jake.

"I'm not," Burroughs protested.

"You are," insisted Jake.

"I am not."

"Are, too."

"I am not."

"Are, too."

"KNOCK IT OFF!" John yelled, having grown tired of the exchange. "BOTH of you are acting childish. now."

"Jake, it's your bet," Andy added, trying to steer past the current roadblock of disagreement. All he could picture was the brawl on the news truck, and he didn't want that to happen again.

"My bet?" Jake answered. He looked at his cards again and selected two blue chips from his dwindling pile. "Here, he offered, tossing them in the center of the table.

"I'm in," Jerry Richards announced, tossing in two blue chips and breaking his silence.

Mike Cummings and Pete Mitchell, George's son, did the same. Warren sat and stared at his cards for an extra minute or two before folding. John threw in his chips, and Andy, the last one, folded, too.

"Alright, Jake," John said finally, looking at him grin. "Let's see what ya got."

Jake reluctantly laid his hand down on the table, revealing a royal straight flush in the suit of spades. A chorus of whistles and obscenities broke out around the table.

"Jeeesus," Warren said, eyeing Jake's cards in complete shock. "Why didn't you bet more than that, Jake?" "I dunno. He answered, shrugging his shoulders".

"Maybe if I had, everyone would's got nervous and folded." He immediately threw a stare at Burroughs, who glared back at him. "If I'd bet a lot. I would've scared everyone off and won nothin', right?"

Warren grunted in agreement, while Andy collected the cards to deal. Jake raked in the small pile of chips he'd won, and digging out his pipe from his pocket, filled and lit it.

Marge Burroughs appeared in the kitchen doorway. "Anyone ready for breakfast?" she asked.

"Sure are," Jake replied for the group, beating everyone to a standing position. "Could eat now," horse, right bout now.

Lt. Michael Travers wished he had a horse right about now. The bridge that crossed Miner's Creek was, in fact, passable, but the half-mile stretch of dirt road beyond that preceded the summit road was a nightmare of mud. The cruisers—Traver's in the lead, with four more behind him—were stuck. Traver's car had traversed the bridge and traveled but one or two car lengths when its tires began to dig in. Traver gunned the engine, but that only managed to speed up the process of getting the car stuck. It sat, now, with the tires nearly all submerged, and as it couldn't move, neither could the car behind it.

A tow truck had been called, but because of the weather and the truck being unable to cross the bridge, here. It had to approach from the other direction—and to do that. It had to climb the mountain and go by way of Knicker's Notch. There was just one single road up and down the mountain.

Travers was absolutely beside himself with rage. which did not escape the observation of the other officers. They all sat in their respective cars and waited for the tow truck, watching the minutes tick by...and tick off the boss.

Travers sat in the driver's seat of his cruiser, sharing his bad mood with Sgt. Peterson, his passenger. Peterson had chosen to ride with Travers rather than use his own cruiser, and now, he was beginning to wish he hadn't.

"Get on the radio and find out where the hell that tow truck is," Travers ordered.

"I just called, Mike, a few minutes ago," Peterson replied.

"I don't care." Travers snapped. "Just do it!"

Peterson reached for the radio's microphone again.

George Mitchell splashed more cold water on his face, then wiped it dry with a towel. He tried to stretch a little but discovered rather quickly that his back didn't like it. He winced a bit, then turned and decided to have a look out the bathroom window. It seemed as if the rain had let up during the last two hours. He pulled back the curtain and squinted to see if he was right.

The first thing he saw was the headlights coming up Jake's driveway. He didn't bother to question whose they were, though. He simply bolted out of the bathroom to go find Jake.

He stumbled down the hall and burst into the kitchen, where most everyone had gathered for breakfast. "Jake!" he yelled, startling everyone. "Someone's outside!'

"What? Who?" Jake replied, the forkful of eggs stopping halfway to his mouth.

"I dunno," George answered, pausing for a breath, "I just save 'em pull in the driveway when I was in the bathroom.

"Lights," Stephanie said. simply.

"What?" someone asked.

"The lights!" she repeated, a hint of panic creeping into her voice. "Shut off the lamps!"

Andy Pierce spun around and ran down the hall to the living room, where the men had been playing poker. He sought out the four lamps in that room and extinguished their flames immediately. The three in the kitchen were turned out at once by those standing next to them. A solid moment of silence followed, as every soul seemed to hold their breath in anticipation. It was Jake who broke the silence. "Now what do we do?" He whispered to no one in particular.

"Why don't you go look out the window and see if you can tell who it is, Jake?" Stephanie answered.

He made his way across the kitchen and disappeared into the darkness of the hallway. Thirty seconds later he reappeared, a shadow in the kitchen doorway. "It's Virgil. He announced.

"Virgil?" Karen Jordan asked. "Who's Virgil?"

"Virgil Parks," George replied. "He owns towing company over in Jericho."

"Why do you think he's here, Jake?" Raren asked.

"I don't know," answered Jake, "he's only stopped up a couple times before."

The loud banging on the front door made everyone jump, though no one moved to answer it.

"Maybe he's workin' for the police."

"Do you think he knows anything?" Burroughs asked.

"Virgil ain't workin' for anybody but himself," Jake responded irritably. "Maybe he heard somethin', but he sure ain't workin' for the police."

"I hate to tell you this, Jake," Karen Jordan explained, "but. Mister Parks is the one our station calls for towing. I recognize the last name. Park's."

The banging persisted, making everyone grow that much more nervous.

"Which means what?" George inquired. "Is he here to tow your cruiser?"

"First, it's not here." Karen answered.

It had been parked behind the store since they'd arrived.

"And?" Jake prodded.

"Well, he ain't here in the middle of a MONSOON for a social visit," George snapped. "He's here looking for you, Jake. I say, You go and find out what he wants."

"I agree," Stephanie said.

The pounding on the door grew louder, as Virgil apparently had no intentions of giving up.

"He KNOWS someone's here, Karen observed, noting how persistent Virgil was. "Go answer it. Jake."

Jake hesitated a few seconds before disappearing again into the hallway.

"Are you sure that's the right thing to do, Officer?"

It was George Mitchell who asked the question.

"As admitted. matter of fact, sir. I'm not." Karen Jordan

"Fair enough," was van George's response. He decided. there and then, that Officer Karen Jordan wasn't dumb after all. It took guts to admit her uncertainty in front of all these people, and he respected her for that. So what if she couldn't find her flashlight...or her hat.

Jake Karner decided to get straight to the point and not waste any time doing so. He threw open the front door, grabbed Virgil by the arm, and, yanking him inside, slammed the door. "What do you want?" he demanded, not bothering with a greeting.

Virgil Parke was one foot shorter than Jake, who stood just a shade short of b! He was a little man who was scared of everyone and everything, including himself. Jake knew it and knew, too, that Virgil would not hesitate to answer his questions nor plead for mercy, if need be. Putting the fear of God into Virgil from the get-go would be the best way to handle the situation.

Virgil couldn't see Jake—it was too dark—and although it was just after five a.m., the storm prevented the light of dawn from appearing. He squinted to make out Jake in the dark but could not, and he was still reeling from the shock of being manhandled when Jake repeated himself. ads. I asked you, Virgil, he said in a threatening tone. "to tell me what you want."

"Jake," Virgil choked, "Did ya' really have to do that?"

"Yes, Virgil, I did," snapped Jake. "I don't have time for playin' games. Now, answer the question."

"The cops are lookin' for you," Virgil stated.

"Tell me somethin' new, Virgil."

"I heard about what Elsie did," he went on, "and I heard how you busted out of jail, so when they called me, I wanted to warn you."

"Virgil, slow down," Jake ordered, "you're babblin' bullshit so fast, it makes sense." He brushed past the little man, who stepped out of his way without a word. Jake located and re-lit one of the kerosene lamps, as well as his pipe. He turned back to Virgil, who had just caught a glimpse of two faces in the darkened hallway beyond. He had a look of horror on his face, and his curiosity had grown. "Virgil," Jake continued, "now, tell me who called you, why, and what you're doin' up here, on the mountain, in such messy weather."

Virgit's eyes darted towards the faces in the hall first, then back to Jake, who stood waiting impatiently.

"The police called me 'bout an hour ago," Virgil complained, checking his watch. "They need me to go and pull one of their cars out of the mud down at the creek. I had to come by your house to get down there, so I thought you might want to know they'll be coming up soon."

Jake absorbed the information and eyed Virgil cautiously, unsure if he was on the level. "How come you came this way?" Jake asked. "Jericho is a stone's throw from the creek."

"The cruiser's stuck just this side of the bridge." Virgil replied, "And there's a bunch more right smack behind it. Couldn't get to it from the other direction."

Jake thought about that, too, for a moment, puffing on his pipe and rubbing the stubble on his unshaven chin. "How long before you get' 'em out of the mud?" he finally asked.

Virgil shrugged. "Depends. I don't know how stuck the car is or how bad the road is down there."

Jake reviewed the options he had available, which weren't many, nor were they promising. He needed to think about things. "Did you have breakfast?" He finally asked.

"Uh, well, no." Virgil stammered, confused by the sudden change of subject. "Didn't have time."

"You want some? Jake offered...

"Well, yeah," Virgil replied, "but what about them cruisers? They're waitin' for me."

So. Let 'em."

"Let 'em what?"

"Let 'em wait," Jake said, casually. "Have yourself somethin' to eat before you go."

Virgil was a small man, but certainly not stupid. He realized what Jake was up to and ventured a smile.

"What's on the menu?" He inquired. "I'm starved."

Jake merely gestured for him to follow him towards the kitchen.

Chapter 16

Muddy Waters

"It's one fine mess you're in," Virgil summed up. shaking his head and wiping his mouth with a napkin. "So, you're just gonna hold up here and wait 'til the cops get here, huh?"

Jake merely nodded and took Virgil's plate and utensils.

"Unless you have a bright idea," he replied.

"Sorry, Jake, but I don't," answered Virgil apologetically. "You're up the old creek with no paddle." He looked at his watch, tilting it towards the light of the lantern. "Speakin' of creeks, I gotta get down there and pull them out," he observed. "That lieutenant sounded real mad, as it is."

"Must be Travers," Stephanie assumed aloud. "The one we tied up."

"Yeah?" Virgil said, "Well, if I don't get there soon,. Someone will have to tie him down again, or he'll have my head."

Everyone in the kitchen shared a laugh or two as Virgil and Jake headed for the front door. Jake paused before opening it up to speak to Virgil. "I want ta' apologize for the way I answered the door before, Virgil. He mumbled, rather embarrassed".

"Don't worry 'bout it, Jake. I understand."

"Thanks, Virg." Jake said, extending his hand.

"Yer' welcome," replied Virgil, shaking the hand. "I just wish there was more I could do to help."

"Just take your time pullin' out that car, Virgil," Jake responded, opening the door to a gust of wind and rain.

"I'll do my best," he promised, and with that, Virgil slipped outside and was gone.

Jake pushed the door closed against the wind and turned to find Burroughs waiting in the center of the living room. "Now what in hell are we gonna do?" he demanded of Jake. Jake wandered across the room and headed for the kitchen. "Time for another town meetin', Burr."

Burroughs followed.

Dawn finally came to Knicker's Notch, if you could call it that. It was still raining hard and much more windy than before. Breakfast had been eaten and the kitchen area cleared to allow all room enough for a meeting. The group had spent nearly an hour discussing their options, and several times, the discussions turned into screaming matches. Every one of those heated arguments included, as one of the disagreeing parties, Jake Warner. George Mitchell had been assigned "watch duty," which placed him in the bathroom for the duration to watch for the police. His being there for that amount of time stirred up trouble, too, as anyone needing to use the bathroom had to plead, beg, or argue to do so. If you were fortunate enough to convince George it WAS an emergency, you still had his self-imposed time limit. He stood outside the door waiting for you to do your thing, and when your allotted one minute and thirty seconds had passed, George promptly began to bang on the door and yell. Miriam tried to stop her husband from doing this to every poor soul who had to "go," but she failed. He even did it to her when she was forced to use the facilities. George's "watch" turned into a nightmare for the others, and he would have continued his reign of terror over the toilet had Jake, himself, not had to use it as well.

George's mistake was treating Jake like the others. Jake didn't take too kindly to George telling him what to do, as it was. The fact that George was ordering him out of HIS OWN bathroom only added to Jake's anger.

George waited the one minute and thirty seconds, then promptly launched into his song and dance of pounding on the door and yelling.

Jake threw open the door and did exactly as he'd done to Virgil. He grabbed George's arm and dragged him inside, shutting the door. He spun around to face George, who, like Virgil, was too shocked to respond at first.

"Who in hell do you think you are?" Jake nearly screamed. "This is MY bathroom!"

"I know that, Jake," George sputtered, "but I gotta keep an eye on the driveway, remember?"

"Yeah, I remember," replied Jake, "but you can't tell people they gotta go in such a short period of time...it ain't right."

"But..."

"NO 'but's, George," Jake interrupted, "Let people do their thing in peace, will ya'?" The question was more of an order, which George didn't want to obey. He stood looking at Jake without saying a word.

"Truth is,. George," Jake added, "when the cops do get here, we'll know right off. There'll be more than one car, and I'll bet all the lights will be flashin."

George took a couple of steps backward and seated himself on the edge of the tub. "You're right," he mumbled. "I'm sorry, Jake."

"Don't worry 'bout it," answered Jake. "I'm done in here now. So go ahead and keep watchin'. Just leave everyone in peace when they're in here, ok? No more of this yellin and stuff."

George nodded. "I'll stop." He resembled a child having been just caught and punished for something. He sat on the tub's edge, staring at the floor.

That is where he was when Jake left the bathroom.

Virgil pulled his tow truck off to the right and reluctantly allowed the stream of cruisers to pass. He'd done everything he could to stall them, but he couldn't do so any longer. "I hope you're ready, Jake," he observed aloud, as the last one passed, " 'cause ready or not, here they come."

"Then that's that," Jake concluded. "It's settled. We'll just sit tight and see what happens."

"Mister Warner," I think it's obvious what will happen, Cheryl Martin said uneasily. "Given the circumstances and evidence, we're all gonna get busted. Period."

Trooper Karen Jordan wanted to throw something at her best friend. She never seemed to listen. "Cheryl," she screamed across the room, "there isn't any evidence! Don't you listen? Stephanie saw to that little problem, so it's Traver's word against our's."

"And I don't think he wants to arrest every one of us, all over again," Stephanie added. "Steve Drever said he'd warn Traver's, and rest assured, if he doesn't listen, Drewer WILL go after him."

"Speakin' of lawyers," Burroughs said from behind Jake, "Did it ever occur to anybody to call one?"

"Burr," Jake replied, twisting in his seat to face his friend, "it's Sunday, remember? What lawyer is gonna answer the phone on a Sunday?"

Burroughs hesitated just a couple of seconds before he answered, "Doctors answer, no matter what time or day it is."

Jake rolled his eyes and turned back to face the group. "Just remember, too." Karen added with a grin. "There are more of us than him."

Everyone was startled by the tone of voice she used. It sounded like a threat, which was, in fact, how Karen had meant it.

"So," Cheryl challenged.

"So," Karen continued, "what happened last time you outnumbered him?"

"He lost," Andy Pierce mumbled.

"Right," Stephanie said, folding her arms and smiling.

"AND," she added proudly, "he ate Elsie's undies."

Only a jackass would set himself up again like that, she thought to herself.

"We wait then," Jake repeated.

Jake then got up and left the kitchen.

Travers rolled down the driver's side window a few inches to converse with one of his officers. "Well?" he asked, yelling over the sound of thunder.

"They're not here, sir," the young officer responded, shuddering with a chill from the wet clothing he now wore. "I can SEE that!" Travers screamed back. "ANY signs of 'em around?"

"None we've found," the trooper responded, "but Sanborn is checking out back and..."

His report was interrupted by a crackle from the radio. Traver's eyes darted to the sound's source, and he waited impatiently for what was next.

"SEVEN, this is TWO," a voice called. Traver recognized it instantly and snatched at the microphone. "Go ahead, Sanborn," Travers ordered, skipping the formalities.

"I've located the news truck and a cruiser out back," he reported, "though there are no signs of anybody around."

Travers was already out of the cruiser and running for the back of the store before he'd finished.

Elsie found her husband nestled in his favorite armchair in their bedroom. It was an old, brown recliner that she'd bought him years ago. It was showing its age, with stains where things had been spilled upon it and spots where Jake's elbows had worn down the material. It wouldn't bring in a buck, even if set out at a yard sale, but it never would be anyhow. It was Jake's favorite, and he wouldn't sell it for all the money in the state of Vermont.

He was puffing on his pipe and staring out the window when she entered the room and shut the door behind her. He turned to see who his visitor was and smiled when he found out it was her. He was always glad to see her, of course, and it was a bigger treat to see her not wearing that horrible apron that clashed with everything she owned.

He removed the pipe from his mouth, and turning it over, he tapped the contents into the ashtray beside him. He proceeded to refill it, wanting a fresh batch of tobacco. Elsie approached rather timidly, and Jake noted her behavior out of the corner of his eye.

"What's the matter, Else?" he questioned, not taking his eyes off his task. "Besides the obvious, that is."

"I wanted to ask ya somethin, Jake," she replied, sitting down on the edge of the bed, just a foot or so away. "We haven't had the chance to talk since all this happened."

Jake grumbled a bit, acknowledging her statement. "I know, it's crazy 'round here with all these people. And imagine George telling' ME to get out of MY OWN bathroom!"

"He means well," Elsie said, coming to George's defense. She straightened her skirt, needing something to occupy her nervous hands.

"Did you?"

"Did I what?"

"Mean well? Did you mean well when you shot Mister Doyle in the back end?"

"I didn't shoot him on purpose," Elsie replied immediately. "THAT was an accident. I fell."

"I still don't know what you were tryin' to do. Else,"

Jake admitted, relighting his pipe.

Elsie sorted through her thoughts for an explanation, coming up empty.

"Did you think Mister Doyle was gonna hurt me or somethin' like that?" He asked.

"Somethin' like that," Elsie replied. "You were so mad, Jake," she explained further, "that I thought he was arrestin' you."

"And what 'bout the truck?" Jake asked.

"What about it?"

"What about it?" Jake repeated, gawking at her. "You mean you don't know what I'm referrin' to?"

Elsie paused a few seconds to reflect, then "Oh, THAT."

"Yeah, THAT, ACKNOWLEDGED, meaning the fight." "What in Heaven's name did you attack Jerry for?" Jake stared at his spouse, waiting for the reason, which he knew already did not exist. Elsie fixed her eyes upon her hands, which lay shaking in her lap. She didn't know what to say.

"Are you mad at me, Jake?" she managed finally.

"Hell no, Else." He leaned over and placed his big hand over hers to reassure her. "I love ya', no matter what. Just stop and think, from now on, b'fore ya' go pullin' people's hair or grabbin' my shotgun. Ok?" He squeezed her hands beneath his to gain a response.

Elsie's eyes came up from her lap to meet his, and she smiled. "Ok," she agreed.

"Alright, then," Jake said, retrieving his hand. "What is it you were gonna ask me?"

"Are we gonna go to jail again?"

"Not if I can help it," Jake replied firmly.

"Damn."

Travera stood in the center of the floor, inside the Channel 12 News truck. Not one of the Knicker's Notch gang was present, of course, and there wasn't a clue left as to where they'd all disappeared to. Travers was angered by that and baffled, too. There appeared to be a great deal of damage to some of the equipment around him. It wasn't the sort of damage that would occur by accident. He was relatively sure there'dn a fight, as things had been knocked around and broken.

The "why" drove him bonkers. He was standing there, amidst the mess of broken glass and his own confusion. thoughts, looking for a clue that wasn't there.

"Sir," a voice called from the open, rear doors. "Sir, Sergeant Feterson would like to speak with you."

Travers nodded and waved a hand to acknowledge the message, and the officer disappeared from view.

"Damn," Travers swore again, then turned to exit.

Sgt. Peterson was seated, in the driver's side, of Trooper Jordan's cruiser, doing the same as Travers had been doing in the news truck—shaking his head and cursing. Travers opened the passenger door and slid in beside him.

"Did you find anything?" Peterson queried, after Travers had slammed the door shut.

"Just a lot of broken junk," Travers answered. "There was some sort of fight in that truck. That much, I'm sure of."

"A fight?" Peterson said doubtfully. "What makes you so sure about that?"

"If they'd stopped fast or somethin', one or two items could've gotten broken, falling off a shelf or whatever, he explained, wiping the rain from his face with a Dunkin' Donuts napkin". From the way things got broken up inside that truck, it had to be during a real, knock-down, drag-out fight. Stuff got knocked over and fell off the shelves, and equipment was damaged. Travers paused to rub his eyes and clean his glasses with the napkin before going on. "It was a fight, alright. Believe it."

Peterson chewed on that information, then combined it. it with what little he knew. "I have a theory," he finally said. "It may not wash with you. I mean, you may not agree, but I'd like to run it by you. Ok?"

"Sure. Dan," Travers replied, his curiosity aroused. "At this point, I don't consider anything impossible, so run it by me. I'm all ears."

Peterson took a deep breath and let out an enormous sigh. "Alright," he warned, "here goes. First, Trooper Jordan has disappeared, along with the group. She was seen leading the truck up here by Sanborn, yes, but she's now among the missing. She never reported seeing the group, just that the bridge was nearly impossible. A false report, I might add. You with me so far?" He waited for Travers to nod that he was. "Ok. You say there was a brawl in the back of that truck, or it LOOKS like there was. I'm putting the pieces together, and I see it like this. Trooper Jordan was wrestled into the back of that truck against her will, and someone else drove her cruiser up here with the truck. I say, when they tried to get out of the truck, Jordan put up one hell of a fight, and that's how stuff got broken. In short, she was kidnapped, and they left the vehicles here to hold up somewhere nearby."

"You think she was forced into going with them," Travers concluded, "and forced to make that report to prevent us from coming up here."

"That's exactly what I think, Mike," Peterson replied, confidently. "Karen Jordan is a good cop, and this doesn't make no sense. The ONLY thing that does is her being kidnapped. She's strong as hell, too," he added, recalling a self-defense class in which Karen had nearly put him in the hospital. "She could and would've put up a real fight. I suspect that's how the damage got done."

Travers removed his glasses and rubbed his eyes again. He turned over the facts, time and time again. and finally came to his own conclusions. "I think you're right, Dan."

"Now that we have a theory, we gotta prove it," Peterson stated, "and we have to figure out where they are to do that."

"The last place I'd look," Travers mumbled, almost inaudibly.

"Huh?"

"I said, they're in the last place they think I'd look," Travers repeated.

"Where's that?" Peterson asked.

"Where this whole nightmare began," Travers replied.

"Warner's house."

Chapter 17

CASUALTIES AND CHAOS

"He must be insane. Cheryl announced, hanging up the phone and turning to Karen. "Absolutely, entirely, and undeniably insane."

"Who?"

"Who else but the one who signs my paycheck?" Cheryl replied.

"Simmons?" Karen asked.

"You should spit when you say his name," Cheryl said. "Yes, Simmons. The one and only. She wandered to the sink to pour a glass of water. After downing the entire glass, she refilled it and turned back to face Karen, who waited for her to explain the phone call.

"He wants me to do a story, with interviews and the whole 'kit an' kaboodle," she continued.

"So, what's the problem?" Karen asked, sipping her mug of hot chocolate. She didn't really understand why Cheryl was so upset, considering it was the story of the decade, and she had the exclusive.

"The problem is, dearie, he wants it done LIVE," Cheryl answered, placing the emphasis on the last word. "He's willing to go on the air at a moment's notice. All I have to do is set up the equipment and yell 'action!'"

"LIVE?" Karen repeated, unsure she'd heard the word for real.

"LIVE."

"He's out of his mind, Cheryl. The minute you go on the air, the cops will be on this place, like spots on a Dalmation."

"I know that, Karen," she snapped, "and I tried to explain that to him, but he didn't hear a single word I said. He said, 'Do it,' and hung up."

"So, what are ya gonna do?"

"Go get the equipment," she replied, placing her glass on the counter. "I'll tape the interviews and a feature piece, and that's it. He'll have to either take it and use it or take it and—well, he'll just have to be happy with it."

"You need help with the equipment?" Karen offered, starting to move as if to help.

"No," Cheryl replied, "that's what Jerry's for. I'm not even sure if the cameras are still working after the fight in the truck. A lot of stuff got broken."

"Did you tell him about that?" Karen asked.

"Are you nuts, too?" Cheryl shot back, astonished. "He'd have my head served at the next budget meeting on a platter."

Cheryl wandered towards the kitchen doorway, then paused to add, "One thing is reassuring, though."

"Oh yeah, what's that?" asked Karen.

"I won't be the only one out of a job when this is over."

Karen didn't find that quite as funny as Cheryl did. who laughed all the way to the front door.

Travers decided to have all the houses checked before he descended on Warner's. He wanted to be certain that the gang was not spread out or congregating somewhere. other than Jake's. He'd been laughed at more than enough already to make that mistake. Travers and Peterson waited in Karen Jordan's cruiser for the units to report in. Sanborn was assigned to check both Warner's and Mitchell's houses. He reported, however, to Traver's dissatisfaction, that Warner's house was empty—or appeared to be from the road—and he proceeded the half-mile down to George Mitchell's. He pulled in the driveway, scanned George's house as well, and reported that it, too, seemed empty. Traver's reply was "Check again, especially Warner's," so Sanborn did, only this time he got out of his cruiser and peered in the windows at George's.

George pulled the curtain aside and scanned the area, as usual. He noted the trees had lost most of their leaves to the high winds and rain, and that saddened him a bit. Autumn had barely arrived, and now, the wonderful colors were gone.

He leaned against the window, placing his elbows on the sill and resting his chin in his hands. Some sort of tiny bird flew by, towards his house, and he pressed his nose against the glass to watch its flight.

That's when he noticed the police cruiser parked in his driveway.

Sanborn walked around the outside of the house and checked the back door before he was ORDERED back to his cruiser. Travers was much more interested in what might be seen through Jake Warner's windows.

Cheryl had her hand firmly planted on the front doorknob when George Mitchell came down the hall yelling bloody murder. The effect was about the same as one might get. yelling "FIRE!" in a crowded theater. Only no one headed for the exits. They just scattered and ran around with no real clue where to go at all. Jake came out of his bedroom and grabbed George by the shoulders, shaking him forcefully to calm him down. That accomplished, he made a split-second decision.

"EVERYONE LISTEN UP!" he yelled for attention. "STOP!"

The chaos died down, but it took a minute or so. With all eyes and ears directed at Jake, he continued. "Everyone in the basement, the door is in the kitchen. NOW!"

He didn't need to say it twice.

Chuck Sandborn was getting uglier by the minute, not to mention wetter, too. He had his full-length rain slicker on and his trooper's hat (enclosed in plastic), but after all this time spent outside, he was damp all over and freezing his former Arizonian butt off. He grew up in Arizona's hundred-degree heat and lived in it almost all of his thirty-four years on this earth. Vermont and its climate had been an enormous shock to his system—a shock he'd yet to recover from. He'd moved here. A mere eight months ago, and now, wet and miserable, he wondered what it would cost him to catch the next plane home.

He pulled his cruiser up behind Doyle's Chevy Blazer, still parked behind Jake's truck. He turned off the motor and sat for a moment, listening to the sound of the rain hitting the car roof. Ironically, he found it to be quite relaxing. The only intrusion was that of the voices on the radio. He reached for the microphone, cleared his throat, and pressed the transmit button. "SEVEN, this is TWO, over."

"Go ahead," Peterson acknowledged, obviously wanting him to get to the point.

"I'm at the Warner place," Chuck reported, wearily. "Looks empty, but I'll check it out and let you know."

He didn't even wait for the response. Instead, he switched off the radio, removed his hat, and stretched a bit. He then closed his eyes and took his morning break.

He deserved it, after all, and what the hell, he thought, Travers won't know....

"What's he doing now?" Jake whispered in Stephanie's ear.

"I'm not sure," she answered, trying to see over Karen Jordan's shoulder. "Karen, what's he doing?"

Karen squinted, trying to see inside the cruiser from her vantage point, but the rain was making it very difficult. She, Stephanie, and Jake had crowded into the bathroom to view the events unfolding outside from the window. It looked out on to the front yard and gave a wide view of it and the driveway as well. Jake's bathroom was rather small: walking in, a small counter preceded the sink and toilet to the left, with a tub/shower on the right, directly opposite the toilet. There was just one window—a small one—so each had to wait their turn to have a look outside.

"Well, Karen?" Stephanie was growing impatient.

"What's he doing?"

"Sanborn, you lazy son-of-a..." Karen's voice trailed off. "Here," she said, stepping to the right enough. to allow Stephanie in. "See for yourself."

Stephanie squeezed in next to Karen and peered outside, wondering why she sounded so disgusted. After a moment, she turned to Karen and said, "He's not doing anything."

"I KNOW THAT, Karen snapped. "That's the point; he's not doing anything. He's just sitting there."

"Well, that's good, ain't it?" Jake asked.

"If he just sits there, yes," Karen replied. "But, he may be waiting for the rest of the gang to get here."

"The gang?" Jake asked. "They're in the basement, remember?"

"NOT our group," Stephanie explained. "She means the rest of the police."

"Oh, was all Jake could manage. He couldn't understand why folks didn't say what they meant. It was so confusing when they didn't use the right words. If she meant police, she should'a said police, not gang....

"Mind if I have a look, too?" Jake asked.

"There isn't much to see, but go ahead…"

Stephanie said, stepping aside for Jake.

Karen didn't expect her move, and Stephanie never looked. Karen stumbled backwards, but there was no place to go, and as she lost her balance, she grabbed on to Stephanie. Both of them tumbled into the bathtub screaming. Stephanie actually screamed twice, but Karen only heard her the first time. It was the last thing she heard before the "lights" went out.

Sanborn's eyes opened and darted in the direction of Warner's house. He'd heard something, though he wasn't sure just what. He looked the house over again, contemplating getting out and ACTUALLY checking out the house. He shivered again in his damp clothing and decided against the idea.

He was, after all, on a break.

"Oh! Oh God! Help me up!" Stephanie pleaded, reaching for Jake's outstretched hands.

"How in the hell did you two..." he was saying as he made an attempt to pull her out. He gave one good yank, and Stephanie was up on her feet. She instantly began to rub the back of her head. "Oh my God, my head," she groaned, "and my back. Oh God, my back hurts."

Jake leaned over to get a closer look at Karen, who was lying in a heap in the tub. "Officer Jordan?"

No answer.

"Officer Jordan, are you ok?"

No response. Stephanie began to panic, so she pushed Jake aside and took a look herself. "Karen, dammit, are you alright?"

Nothing.

"You killed her," Jake announced, stunned by the mere words themselves.

Stephanie opened her mouth to reply, but she couldn't find her voice.

"You killed her," he repeated, turning to face Stephanie. "Lord in Heaven, help us all. Don't you think we've got enough problems 'round here? Now, we've got a dead body too."

Chapter 18

NO NAME

"See, I told you, she's not dead," Stephanie said. setting Karen's wrist is down. "She's got a pulse. She's just unconscious, Mister Warner."

"Well, thank the Lord for that," he replied, breathing a sigh of relief. "Had me scared there for a second."

"Me, too," she admitted, eyeing Karen for a moment. "Well, now, we gotta get her out of here," she went on.

"But, then what?"

Jake looked at Karen, too. Poor kid, he thought....

She's gonna have one helluva headache later...

"Let's pull her out and bring her downstairs in the basement," he suggested. "Then we'll have to figure out what to do next."

"Mister Burroughs can check her out," Stephanie said, recalling he was a physician.

"Yeah, good idea," Jake answered, smiling. "You're pretty smart, ya' know that?"

"Some days I am," she replied, "and then there are days I act like I haven't got a brain in my head."

"I don't believe that, Miss Wilson. You DID figure out how to get us out of jail and planned it all. We're all grateful for that."

Stephanie nodded. "Like I said before, Mister Warner. It was my pleasure to help you folks out. Now, go get some help so we can get Karen out of here. I'll keep an eye out the window, ok?"

Jake nodded and left the bathroom.

Chuck opened his eyes and checked his watch. Nearly twenty minutes had passed since he'd turned off the radio for his unauthorized break. He decided he'd better check in before Travers had a coronary. He switched it on and was instantly assaulted by his superior's voice, calling his name and demanding an answer. Chuck cleared his throat and pressed the button. "This is Sanborn, over."

"WHERE THE HELL HAVE YOU BEEN?" Travers bellowed. "I've been calling for twenty minutes!"

"I was checking out the barn," sir, he lied, suppressing a smile. "It's big and dark and a great hiding place. I wanted to be thorough, sir."

"Why didn't you take your radio?" Travers demanded…

"Forgot, sir." Chuck replied, thinking about that plane ticket home again.

"Well, forget the barn," Travers ordered. "I want that house checked now, and I want it done thoroughly, too."

"Yessir," he replied, "and I'll report back as soon as it's done. Sanborn, out."

He turned the radio off, again, before Travers could respond.

This whole Knicker's Notch mess was a joke, anyhow. He had gotten most of the pertinent details, and he couldn't understand why Travers was so hell-bent on catching these people. He looked at the house again, wondering if, in fact, they were inside. He saw no movement, nor anyone peering out the windows at him. The shades weren't all drawn, as if to prevent someone from seeing inside, and except for the unusual sound a few minutes ago, nothing seemed out of the ordinary or enough to raise his suspicions. He didn't really feel like wandering around in the rain anymore, yet. Travers would hold him responsible if they were here, and he missed them. Not checking the house out could cause more problems than his wet clothing could. He thought it over for another moment before making his decision. Finally, he sighed, muttered an obscenity, and reached for his hat.

It was time for another walk in the rain.

Stephanie wished Karen would come around, as it would be far easier to help an injured person move than a hundred pounds or so of dead weight. She looked at Karen again for signs of movement but found none. Karen was out cold. She turned her attention back to the cruiser in the driveway, just in time to see the door open. "Oh shit," she swore, watching the trooper get out. "Now, we're in it, for sure."

Chuck slammed the door shut and walked around the front of his cruiser. He had to hold his hat on his head; the wind was blowing so hard. He decided to begin at the back of the house, so he crossed the lawn and disappeared from view. Stephanie's view—that is, Stephanie panicked, of course. She spun around and searched for a large towel or something to cover Karen with. The trooper would see Karen the moment he looked in the bathroom window. Stephanie wasn't even sure he would, but she wasn't going to try her luck. So far, it wasn't on her side. Failing to locate a towel, she yanked the shower curtain closed, which covered Karen sufficiently from view. She almost pulled the shade but decided against it. The trooper would more than likely recall it had been up, and then, something was strange.

Stephanie slipped out of the bathroom and down the hallway, towards the kitchen. She prayed Jake was still in the basement, not standing in the kitchen. The trooper was probably looking in those windows at this very moment.

She was passing the hall closet when she was suddenly grabbed from behind. One hand seemed to be pulling her backwards, while the other stifled her shriek.

It happened so quickly, she didn't have time to react. And in a matter of seconds, she was crammed into the closet with the door shut.

"Relax," the voice whispered. "It's me, Jerry. Don't scream, alright?" Stephanie nodded, and Jerry then removed his hand from her mouth. "Sorry," he apologized, "but the cop is out back." "I know," she replied, "I saw him headed that way."

It was pitch black in the closet, and the smell of mothballs was beginning to make Stephanie sick to her stomach. She turned in the direction of Jerry's voice and tried to breathe through her mouth, not her nose. "I pulled the shower curtain so he won't see Karen in the tub."

"Now, that was real smart of ya'," Jake whispered, startling her.

"Jeeeeesus," she exclaimed, feeling her heart pounding in her chest. "Mister Warner, you scared me. I didn't know you were in here, too."

"Sorry 'bout that," he muttered.

"Anybody else here?" Stephanie asked them both.

"No," Jerry answered, "just us."

"Ain't any more room in here, anyhow," Jake added.

"Good," Stephanie said, accidentally breathing through her nose. She swallowed hard to settle her stomach, but it kept sending up that horrible, acidic taste.

"We do what we've been doin'," Jake replied. "We wait."

"Now what?" Jerry asked aloud.

"Yeah," added Stephanie. "And pray, too."

Lilies. No, daisies. They were daisies, and big ones, too, set against a faded, pink background.

Karen decided it was the ugliest thing she'd laid eyes on. Since seeing Elsie's dress and apron, anyway. She thought THOSE were awful, but this was worse. This shower curtain was actually painful to look at, so she closed her eyes.

She never questioned where she was, nor even why she was there. It hurt too much to think.

Chuck saw no one in the kitchen, so he moved on. Peering in the bedroom window, he found the same to be true. Nobody around. He ducked under the cover of the back porch and dug his radio out of his pocket. He turned it on and pressed the transmit button. "SEVEN, this is TWO, over."

"Go ahead, TWO," came Peterson's reply. "What did you find?"

"Nothing, yet, sir," Chuck answered, relieved to be speaking to someone other than Travers. "I just looked in the kitchen and bedroom windows and saw no one around."

There was a pause, of ten seconds or so, before Peterson spoke again. "Make sure those rooms are empty before. You check the rest," he ordered, "and check the barn again."

"Yessir," Chuck replied. "I'll check back when that's done."

He switched off the radio and put it back in his pocket. realizing for the first time how soaked his feet were. Looking down, he saw them covered with mud. "Terrific," he muttered, "and now, I can go and get cowshit on 'em, too."

"I need some air, Jerry," Stephanie said, a hint of desperation present in her voice. "I'm getting claustrophobic."

"I don't know where that cop is, Steph," he replied. "He might see you in the hall."

"You can't see into the hall from outside," Jake informed him. "She can stand outside the closet, and she'll be fine. He won't see her."

"Jerry, please," Stephanie pleaded. "I'm gonna puke, if I don't get outta here quick."

"Alright," he conceded, "but stay right outside this door, ok?"

"Yes, yes, now open it, will ya?"

Jerry carefully opened the door, and Stephanie all but shoved him out of the way, getting out.

Daisies? Why daisies? Why not happy faces or a rainbow? Why daisies, and such big ones, in such an ugly pattern on such a horrible color?

Karen didn't understand, and as she tossed around the

"Whys," she noticed something else. The curtain clashed with the wallpaper.

She groaned aloud and closed her eyes again.

Chuck climbed back into the cruiser and removed his hat. He'd decided not to bother with the barn or any of the other rooms, for that matter. He was soaking wet. and he'd found nothing. The only things he'd seen were the usual objects found in a home. He saw no people. Not a single soul. Just furniture, lamps, lanterns, and some clothes lying around.

He started to reach for the microphone when it occurred to him. "Lanterns?" he asked aloud. He recalled seeing them in the kitchen, too.

He'd also seen camping stoves on the counter.

"Well, well, well," he said, a smile spreading across his face. "Looks like Bonnie and Clyde and company ARE here."

The question was, of course, what to do about it.

Chapter 19

WHEN IT RAINS, IT POURS

"SEVEN, this is Dispatch, over."

"Go ahead, dispatch; this is unit seven," Travers acknowledged, wishing it were Sanborn reporting in.

"The Weather Service has just issued an update on Hurricane Rita," the female voice stated.

"Hurricane?" Travers replied, "What hurricane? That was downgraded to a depression or storm, wasn't it?"

"It was downgraded at oh-two-thirty, this date,"

She confirmed, answering his request. "But certain conditions have upgraded it again. They do stress that it is not increasing in intensity, rapidly or steadily, and it's a borderline storm, if you will. Barely a hurricane."

"Damnit." Peterson was fumbling with a damp cigarette and weighing this new information against the present situation. He was not a happy camper.

Travers extracted a Parker Roller Ball from his breast pocket and reached for his clipboard. "Dispatch, we're ready for the details, over."

"Weather conditions, as of oh-six-hundred, and recorded at Brattleboro, are as follows," she continued, pausing to take a deep breath. "Hurricane Rita is moving due north at a speed of 23 miles per hour. Her eye is passing over the town of Grafton, and winds are gusting to 80 miles per hour at Brattleboro. The gusts have averaged about seventy to seventy-five, which forced the weather service to upgrade her again. Several tornadoes have been sighted near Brattleboro, and it's raining buckets. Travers smirked when he realized she'd used that old phrase, rather than what the Service had sent out.

"What are they saying it's gonna do now?"

"The Weather Service predicts that Rita will slow down during the next four to six hours," she replied, "and although she will be downgraded to a tropical storm again within an hour or two, they're warning all to take precautions anyway. Winds will continue to gust upwards of sixty miles an hour, and the backside of the storm could drop a funnel cloud or two in the low-lying areas." "Damnit, Peterson swore again, stubbing out his cigarette. "This is just what I need, a..."

"Cool it, Dan," Travers snapped, "Let me get the rest, and then we'll deal with it."

The dispatcher paused, apparently to take care of some other problem on her end, then returned with the rest of the weather bulletin. "This is dispatch," she said, sounding a bit irritated. "Things are busy here. Sorry, sir."

"We're aware of how things are on your end," Travers assured her, "so don't concern yourself. Now, how about the rest of that advisory."

"Service says", she went on, "and this was over an hour ago, that the eye should pass just east of Rutland by eight-thirty. Following that track, it should pass just to the west of Montpelier at around ten."

Travers was scribbling away, trying to get the facts down in a way that he could make sense of them. Peterson opted to take the easy way and had taken out a pen and paper, too. Only he was drawing something. He had remained quiet throughout the latter part of his bosses radio con-versation, but the name "Montpelier" drew another curse from him.

"Dan, what's the problem?" Travers snapped. "This is the third time you've interrupted me with your mouth."

Peterson ignored his boss and friend for another moment, concentrating on the sketch he was making.

Travers leaned over to see what it was he was drawing, but the light inside the cruiser wasn't sufficient. It was daylight now, but the storm decreased that to a dreary. eerie, and a darker shade of grey.

"Daniel," Travers persisted, growing angrier by the millisecond, "You may be a friend, but you are a subor..."

He was interrupted by the sudden thrust of Peterson's drawing into his view--just inches away from his nose. He jumped first, reflexively, and then leaned back to bring the paper into focus. It was a rough drawing of the state of Vermont, with the information just given him over the radio added in. Beginning at the bottom, right, there was the town of Brattleboro, and moving northward, Peterson had added in Grafton, Rutland, Montpelier, and their location. "Yeah, so?" Travers challenged. "You make good maps. so, what's the point. Dan?"

Peterson snatched the paper away and added something else to his map. Five seconds passed, and it was back in Traver's view. Peterson had drawn a line with an arrow. beginning at Brattleboro and moving northward.

Just like Hurricane Rita was moving.

"We're in trouble, Mike."

Rita was coming to visit Knicker's Notch.

Chuck Sanborn had monitored the conversation between his boss and the dispatcher, and came to the same realization simultaneously. He, however, had pulled out a "real" map to refer to. He hadn't been in the state long enough to know where all the towns and cities were. During the pause in transmissions, he'd taken a pen and drawn the line that depicted the track of the storm, and when he'd added the line from Grafton north--the one that would pass east of Rutland--he swore under his breath. You didn't have to be a weatherman to figure out the rest of the story. He'd been hearing about hurricane "Rita" for days, getting snippets from the news. It wasn't until it made landfall, yesterday, that his interest peaked. It had, at its worst, reached a category "4" on the scale of one to five. Storms reaching this severity were rare, and rarely, too, did they follow the track this one had.

This storm had been tricky, though, from the get-go. It shifted every time the weatherman blinked, and even their predictions late last evening had been proven inaccurate to some degree. And with hurricanes, a degree is a lot--miles, to be exact. The weatherman were at "Rita's" mercy, as she glided here and there in the Atlantic and couldn't make up her mind where to go. Thursday, she appeared to make that long-awaited decision, as she shifted gears and darted towards the mainland.

The weathermen up and down the Atlantic seaboard nearly panicked, as now, they had to figure out which state would receive her. She zeroed in on Connecticut and Rhode Island but wandered and wavered just enough to make the residents of both crazy. It was pretty much a given that she would do severe damage to both coastal fronts, so many boarded up and left their homes early in the game. Some didn't bother boarding up at all. They knew their home wouldn't be there when they returned, so they saved the wood and nails "to start building the new house" when it was over.

Chuck had grown up in a state that saw a tornado now and then. Ile understood the pain of losing your home and all you owned. He was just eight years old. when one ripped through his hometown of Chalender. He was in school at the time, and the warning was never sounded. He was adding numbers in math class when the roar was heard.

Everyone dove for the floor, and in moments it was over. It never touched the school, but when Chuck got home, he found he really had no home to come to. The entire neighborhood and everything within a square mile were destroyed.

His older brother Jeremie had been home from school sick, and his mother had gone to the food mart for grocer-les. Jeremie would've been thirteen, in less than a month.

He shuddered, now, trying to shake the unpleasant memory. It was hard to forget the devastation, though. both within his town and his heart. Still, he had to. His gaze travelled across the lawn to the Warner's front door, and he knew, instantly, what he had to do.

The first thing he did, before leaving his vehicle, was remove his badge. Then he started the car and drove it around back of the barn. It was a good place to hide it, out of view of the road.

Chapter 20

RECONNAISSANCE

Despite the pleadings of Jerry and Jake, Stephanie crawled down the hall to check on Karen. She'd heard a sound—something akin to a "groan"—and thought Karen might be regaining consciousness. She crawled into the bathroom and right up to the window, where she peered out to see where the trooper was, first. "Oh my God," she muttered, seeing the cruiser had disappeared.

"It is ugly, isn't it?" A voice mumbled from behind. Stephanie was so wrapped up in her own thoughts that she didn't realize, at first, she was being spoken to. It registered nearly half a minute later.

"Huh?" Stephanie grunted, turning around.

"I said, It's ugly, isn't it?" the voice repeated.

"Karen!" Stephanie nearly yelled, yanking back the shower curtain.

"Hi," Karen managed, adding a faint smile.

Stephanie grinned.

"Well?"

"Well what?" Stephanie replied.

Karen raised her right hand and pointed. "Ain't that ugly?"

"The curtain?"

"Yeah, the curtain," Karen confirmed. "I've been staring at that forever."

Stephanie giggled, relieved that Karen, for the moment, appeared to be alright.

"You ok?" she asked. "Anything broken?"

Karen paused to take inventory, locating and registering everything that hurt, which seemed to be everything. "Nothing's broken," she concluded, smiling again.

"You sure?" Stephanie challenged, "You're white as a ghost."

"I'm ok," Karen assured her, wincing as a pain shot up through her left shoulder.

"You look like a decendent of Death," Stephanie remarked.

"Well, I'm gonna be the daughter of Draino if you don't get me outta here, quick," Karen replied. "Where's that idiot, Sanborn, now?"

"Who?"

"That trooper outside was a guy I work with," Karen explained. "Where is he, now?"

"I wish I knew," Stephanie replied, "He's gone. His cruiser, too."

"Gone? Where?"

"I dunno," Stephanie answered. "He got out to have a look around while you were taking a bath. I pulled the curtain, to cover you in case he looked in here, and I was hiding in the closet. I came out just now."

"I'm honoured you came out of the closet for me," Karen replied, smiling.

"Ha, ha, ha," Stephanie said. "Anyway, he's gone."

"The question is where, then," Karen concluded, "and we'd better find out quick."

Opening the door slowly was taking every ounce of patience George had left. It was creaking, and he was sure it could be heard for miles. He and Warren had been elected to go in search of Jake and the others. George only went willingly because he had to go to the bathroom. Warren had gone just to get out of the ankle-deep water in the basement. The storm had brought quite a bit of rain, all of which, Warren was sure, had gathered in Jake's basement.

George was proceeding with caution, fearing the police were already in the house. Warren was having fits, because he was taking so long to open the door, and George was ready to push him down the stairs. He was about to turn and utter something akin to a death threat when the door was suddenly yanked open from the other side. George froze, unable to move from where he stood. Warren, on the other hand, all but fell down the stairs trying to get away.

Chuck assumed the door would be locked and had armed himself with a crowbar. To his surprise, the back door was unlocked, and he slipped into the kitchen without a sound. He had closed the door and paused to listen for signs of life when he heard it--the creaking of the door that led to the cellar. He wasted no time in finding out who was behind it, pulling it open in a flash. He saw the terrified expression on the man's face and began to explain his actions almost immediately.

"Now, just relax, sir," he said, setting the crowbar down on the floor. "I am NOT here to arrest you or harm you."

George blinked in disbelief and closed his mouth. He swallowed hard, trying to determine how to respond to the trooper.

"My name is Chuck. Chuck Sanborn, and yes, there are a bunch of cops down the road, but I'm the only one who knows you folks are here."

Chuck took a step backwards to give George a bit of breathing room. Perhaps, he thought, he'll feel less threatened. "There is a hurricane due south of here," he went on slowly, "what's left is headed this way, and I wanted to warn you."

"Hurricane?" George repeated, finally finding his voice. "You mean what's-her-face, uh, let's see, her name was..."

"Rita," Chuck replied, relieved the man was, at the very least, speaking to him now. "Yes, that one. It's big and even though it's startin' to wind down, it'll do some damage. I didn't think you knew, with the power out and all."

"We didn't know," George confirmed, shaking his head.

"Didn't hear a thing about that at all." He looked the trooper over and asked, "And you came to warn us?"

"Sure did."

"And you're telling me the truth, now, right?"

"Yes, sir. So help me God." Chuck said, raising his right hand.

"You're not lyin'."

"No."

"For your sake, I hope not, George warned, cause if you are, Elsie's got."

With that, he signalled for Chuck to follow as he turned and went down the stairs.

"Ow! Ow! Ow! Wait! You're hurting' my arm!"

Stephanie had enlisted Jerry's help in getting Karen out of the tub. They'd barely touched her, when she began screaming.

"If you don't keep your voice down, you'll get us thrown in jail again!" Stephanie warned through clenched teeth.

"If you don't watch what you're doing, I'll put you there myself!" Karen shot back, beads of sweat rolling down her cheeks.

"You won't have the authority," Stephanie reminded her with a smile. "'cause you won't have a job."

"Thanks to you, you stupid..."

"STOP IT!" Jerry yelled, startling them both into silence. "Just stop it, right NOW!" His face was nearly purple; he was so angry. Scenes from the brawl on the news truck flashed before his eyes, and coupled with this little sideshow, he wondered, how people could say small townsfolk were so friendly. He shook his head slowly and the confusion showed on his face.

"Are you alright?" Stephanie asked, noting his color and facial expression.

"I'm gonna be ready for the cardiac care unit, de if you two keep at it," he replied. "Don't you think things are bad enough without you two fighting?"

Neither of the two women would meet Jerry's stare, although Stephanie's cheeks turned pink with embarrassment.

"If you want to argue", he went on, "do it later." He looked from Karen to Stephanie and then added, "Please."

Karen reluctantly mumbled a "yes", while Stephanie merely nodded.

"Great," Jerry said, breathing heavily, "Now, let's try this again. Ready?"

"Ready," Karen acknowledged.

"Okay, on the count of three," Stephanie announced.

"One...two...THREE!"

Peterson lowered his window to allow the cigarette smoke out of the stuffy cruiser. He noted that the winds were increasing, and the temperature had actually risen. Travers was busy making notes and trying to figure out how much time he had left. He had no intentions of calling off the search until he absolutely had to. Peterson knew, however, the weather would have to be terribly severe if that were to happen. He wanted to find these people as much as Travers did, now that two of his officers were among the missing. He also wanted to keep the number of those missing to just two--driving around in the middle of a hurricane seemed a fine way to add to that number – and he wanted to express that to Travers.

"Mike", he began nervously, "we need to do something soon."

"I know that," Travers snapped, looking up from his notes to glare at his colleague. "Truth is, I don't know what. We've looked everywhere, but there's no sign of 'em. And I know they're here, Dan. I can feel it."

"Maybe they WERE here," Peterson said, "but now they're gone."

"No, Dan," Travers replied, dismissing the idea immediately. "They're still here and I'll find them. Storm or no storm, I'll get them and haul them all back to jail where they belong."

Sanborn took the basement stairs two at a time, heading for the source of the scream. He'd only reached the bottom step when he'd heard it, and he wasted no time asking George whom it belonged to. Whoever it was, was in pain and in need of help.

George took the stairs as fast as he could, trying to follow the Trooper. The rest of the gang downstairs only stood in shock at first. Marlene was yelling at her husband to come back, while Elsie Warner made attempts to enlist the others into helping out, too. Burroughs argued that the policeman could handle it, but that argument, obviously, was far from being a convincing one. For nearly a minute, everyone merely bickered about what to do next, and it wasn't until Elsie headed for the stairs that a decision was reached.

They all followed, knowing what happens when Elsie gets angry.

Chapter 21

ANYTHING FOR A STORY

Chuck Sanborn came jogging down the darkened hallway too fast, and never saw Jake coming in the opposite dircct-ion. They collided and fell to the floor swearing and making threats to one another.

Karen's first scream was relatively short. It was the second one that took everyone by surprise, nearly shaking the windows. Jerry and Stephanie had tried to be careful in pulling Karen from the tub. They stood there wondering what they'd done to make her scream like that. Jake and Sandborn even stopped their minor brawl in the hallway to take a look.

The question was: Had Karen put weight on an injury and found herself in excruciating pain, or was the sight of the wallpaper and shower curtain clashing, now, driving her over the edge?

They stood and wondered, while Karen kept on screaming.

"Warner's," Travers mumbled, putting the cap on his pen and tucking it in his pocket.

Peterson, caught daydreaming about a hot shower and coffee, turned a weary expression towards his friend and boss.

"What?" he asked.

"Warner's", Travers repeated. He placed the clipboard on the dashboard and reached for the radio mike. "They're all hiding out at Warner's house."

"But.."

Travers raised his hand to quiet Peterson's protests.

"No, Dan," he explained, "Sanborn is either blind or stupid. And it strikes me as awfully funny that he has disappeared, too. He reported that the place was empty and all that, and then, poof! He turned up missing. I think they're up there and all hiding out in the damn basement or something. I also think that they're grabbing anyone that happens to find them. They grabbed your other officer, right? What's her name?"

Peterson had turned his attention to the front door of the store, where one of his officers was peering intently in-side the front window. Something had caught his eye, and Peterson wondered what it was. "Try Sanborn," he half-ordered, opening the cruiser door. "I'll be right back."

The door slammed shut before Travers could argue. Shrugging, he keyed the microphone to transmit and began to call for Sanborn.

Stephanie slapped Karen so hard she nearly knocked her into the bathtub again. "Karen, STOP!" She yelled, "They'll hear you in Burlington, for Chris'sake!"

Karen stared at Stephanie for a few seconds, stunned by the slap. "My arm," she mumbled softly. "My arm, I think it's broken."

Stephanie felt suddenly guilty for having struck her. It was obvious that Karen was in a lot of pain. Her face was white and there were beads of sweat on her forehead. "I'm sorry," she offered. "It's just that screaming like that, my God..."

"The screaming is a way of reducing stress," Karen explained, matter-of-factly. "I learnt that in a..."

Stephanie's mouth dropped open in shock, then, "Stress?" You were screaming bloody murder to reduce stress?!"

Karen simply nodded.

Jerry saw the look on Stephanie's face and knew it was time to interrupt. "Ladies," he began, but he was interrupted and shoved aside by Sanborn.

Chuck apologized half-heartedly and turned to Karen. "Jordan", he said, sounding official, "You alright? What in Hell is going on? What happened here? How did..."

He was distracted by the commotion in the hallway and alerted by the words Jake uttered. "Uh oh" always meant trouble. He moved past Jerry and stepped out into the hall, where Jake was pleading with Elsie.

"Else, it's alright," he was saying, hands raised in a calming gesture. "Miss Jordan hurt herself is all. Now, put the broom down, ok?"

Elsie did not appear convinced, as she shifted her gaze and the end of the broom towards the trooper, now eyeing her.

"Who in hell are you?" she demanded, ignoring her husband for the moment. "How did you get in my house?"

Chuck could not see the faces behind her clearly, only shapes and shadows. Still, he was certain that all were present and quite prepared to back up the woman with the broom.

It was nearly Halloween, but being attacked with a broom didn't fit into the "Trick or Treat category at all. He shifted his gaze back to Elsie Warner and chose his words carefully.

"I am Trooper Charles Sanborn, Ma'am, and I got in through your back door, which was unlocked."

Elsie glanced at her spouse, whose eyes rolled in disgust. She ignored him and looked at the trooper again. "Who said you could come into my house, and where are the rest of your friends?"

"No one gave me permission," Ma'am, Chuck answered.

"I was assigned to check the premises for signs of you folks, for reasons you're already aware of. I figured out you were here but wasn't sure if I was gonna tell anybody." He paused to let that information sink in and to sum up his actions after finding them. He knew that he'd have to prove he was on their side--sort of--and that was not going to be easy. "I was outside, sitting in my cruiser when the dispatcher informed my boss, Lt. Travers, that there was severe weather on the way. In short, the power is out, the weather is bad, and I thought you might like to know they might get worse."

Chuck waited for a response from the broom-toting woman just five feet away, but none came. It was Stephanie who broke the silence.

"So, where's Travers now?"

"Down the road, at the store," Chuck replied immediately. "They've searched Trooper Jordan's cruiser and are searching the new newstruck, too. For clues, of course, as to where you all are."

"Cheryl," came Jerry's voice from inside the bathroom.

Stephanie and Chuck turned to him, confused.

"Cheryl," he repeated, seeing their inquisitive looks.

"Where in the hell is Cheryl?"

"Last I saw her, she was going for the front door with you." Stephanie replied, "just as the cruiser pulled in the driveway. I thought she went for the basement like the rest of the group..."

"I never saw her in the basement," a voice called from the darkened hallway, behind Elsie. "I'm sure of that," Andy added.

"If she isn't here, then where is she?" George asked.

"She couldn't have gone out the front door without being seen."

"She could have gone out the back, Jake replied, "after we all filed down the stairs into the cellar."

"Shit," Jerry swore, shaking his head. "And it was dark enough that we wouldn't have noticed she was missing."

"But why?" Karen asked, cradling her right arm and wincing with every word. "Where would she go and WHY?" No sooner had she asked the question than the answer occurred to her. "Oh my God," she said, shock registering on her face. "She's headed for the truck."

"Why?" Chuck asked. "And that's a helluva walk, too."

"Simmons", Jerry explained, clenching his fists. "He demanded we do a live story, and now she's headed for the truck to get the camera."

"She walked? In this weather?" Sanborn asked, "It's windy as hell out there and raining."

"My guess is", Jake offered in response, "that she didn't walk. There's an ol' three speed bike in the barn. Was my son's when he was small, and she must've found it."

Everyone's mouth dropped open in shock. Elsie's, too, only she dropped the broom at the same time.

"O.K., Flipper, what ya' lookin' at?" Peterson asked, jumping onto the porch to join Lapierre. The wind was whipping his rain slicker in all directions, proving to be useless against the driving rain.

"Well, sir," he replied, "I didn't notice before 'cause it was dark when we got here. Have look," he offered stepping aside.

Peterson would've preferred he just tell him what he'd seen, and the irritation was evident in his face as they exchanged places. He placed his nose to the window and tried to focus on the interior of the store. "I don't see what you do, Flipper, he finally admitted.

"Sir." Lapierre began, "I was in this store a few times this summer, an' I can see that stuff is missing. Look behind the counter, there."

"Yeah, so?"

"Well, sir," he continued, "every last battery and flashlight is missing. Look at the shelves, too. Canned goods, t.p., and the like."

"Someone's been shopping," Peterson announced with a huge grin as he turned to face Lapierre, "and I have a pretty good idea who and why, too."

Flipper returned his bosses' smile.

Neither one would've been grinning if they'd been paying. closer attention.

Cheryl's timing had been perfect, although she hadn't actually planned it that way. She rounded the corner and sped by the store while both troopers were peering in the store window. She'd fought to control the aging 3-speed in the mud that seemed as deep as she was tall. Travers even missed her, rubbing his tired eyes which had grown tired of searching.

He'd even missed, the sight of her skirt blowing up, to kiss her face as she passed.

It fell again just in time to prevent her slamming into the rear bumper of the newstruck.

Cheryl all but fell off the bike and sent it rolling another 10 yards into the tall grass to her left. Satisfied it was concealed, she crouched and made her way to the driver's side door. Cursing Simmons--her psycho boss--the weather, her attire, and the pain in her knee, she opened the door and slid into the driver's seat, unseen. She peered out the passenger window to be sure, spotting only the second cruiser parked on the opposite side of the store. Only its back fender was visible, but she assumed it belonged to one of the troopers in NAS who were standing on the front porch. Once she was convinced that no one had seen her, she settled back in the seat to catch her breath. Against her better judgement, she turned the rear-view mirror towards her to get a look at how awful, she already knew, she must look. Her makeup was now. non-existent. Only the remnants of her mascara remained and it, combined with her wrecked perm and bloodshot eyes, gave her the appearance of the crazed person, she told herself she must be. Doing a live, on-the-air report was crazy. How she was going to get the newstruck back to Warner's unseen was the problem. She couldn't just take a camera and run for it. The power being out left the newstruck's portable generator the only source of electricity. The truck had to be moved. "Now what?" she asked her reflection.

The answer came too easily, she would recall later.

"They ARE at Warner's!" Peterson yelled at Travers, sliding into the cruiser again.

"And what makes you so sure of that, Dan?" Travers replied sarcastically. "I've told you that all a..."

"I needed to be convinced," Dan answered. "And NOW I am. They did some shopping in there. Mike. A LOT of shopping, and they took some very specific items, too."

Travers eyed his friend suspiciously, for a moment.

"Batteries?" he asked.

"All of 'em," Dan replied.

"Flashlights?"

"Uh huh."

"What else?" Travers enquired.

"Canned goods, TP, stuff like that," Dan answered.

"Start the engine, Dan."

"Yes, sir," Peterson responded.

The engine did not.

Cheryl was going too fast and didn't care. She would need a head start, if she had any chance of pulling this off.

Warren would've thrown fits had he seen Cheryl take the corner so close to the store. She barely missed the porch by inches and even managed to do it with her eyes squeezed shut.

Travers and Petersen were peering under the hood of Karen's disabled cruiser, which added insult to injury, as she roared on by. They discovered the distributor cap had been loosened and a couple of wires had been pulled apart. Just enough "sabotage" to render the cruiser useless for a bit.

Travers took off chasing the news van on foot, and got only about ten feet when he slipped and fell in the mud. Petersen ran for LaPierre's cruiser, but "Flipper" was already in motion and nearly ran him down. He left him standing there, waving an angry fist and yelling cuss words he obviously couldn't hear.

"How is she gonna get the equipment back, here, Jerry?" Karen asked, "In her freakin' purse?"

"Calm down, Karen," Jerry pleaded.

He, Karen, and Stephanie had filed down the hall to the kitchen. Jake had gone out to the barn, to see if the bike was, in fact, missing.

"Well, really, Jerry," Karen whined, "you should've stopped her!" "I didn't know she was gonna try something like this!" He shot back.

"Will she try and bring the van back here?" Stephanie interrupted, somehow, already knowing the answer.

Jerry hesitated. "If she can, yes."

"Oh, that's just terrific!" Stephanie shrieked, placing her hands on her hips. "an she'll bring every cruiser in the state, with her! I never should'a asked her to help, knowing she'd do anything for a story!"

"Now, wait one minute," Jerry snapped, coming to his colleague's defense, "I don't think she's THAT stupid..."

"Jerry!" Stephanie screamed, turning red with anger, "She's gone up there, on a ninety-year-old bike, in the middle of a monsoon, for God's sake! Riding right smack into the middle of a Trooper convention! That doesn't sound too swift to me, Jerry!"

"Well, she hasn't completely lost her marbles," Jake offered, coming in the back door. He held up his hand, to show everyone what he'd found. "She had the sense to take off her heels, anyhow." Karen fainted.

Cheryl knew she'd have to make it to Jake's without the pursuing cruiser seeing where she was going. She had no idea what to do with the van once she got there, but that was the least of her problems. She stepped on the gas, taking the corner much too fast. All the equipment, that wasn't secured, went airborne, with something hitting her in the back of the head. She almost lost control, and managed to swerve just enough to the right, to run down George's mailbox.

George was peering out the window and couldn't believe his eyes.

"Uh oh," he muttered.

George spun around and bolted out and down the hall to the kitchen. Jerry, Jake, and Stephanie were trying to revive Karen with a wet towel. He grabbed Jake by the arm, "She's coming!" he screamed.

"What?" Jake replied, "Who's coming?"

"Oh, Lord in heaven," Jake muttered, turning to run for the door.

"She's got the truck!" George yelled.

"Where are you going?" Jerry called after him.

Jake didn't answer.

Cheryl came into the driveway, nearly sideways, and much to her surprise, there was Jake. He was standing by the open barn door, waving frantically for her to drive on in. Swerving around Trevor's Chevy Blazer and Jake's pick-up, she soared into the barn and came to an abrupt halt. Jake yanked the barn door shut, then scurried over to greet her. She took a deep breath, then threw open the door and jumped out, in her bare feet.

Jake looked at her, then down at her feet.

"M'am," he said softly, wiping the rain from his face with a grin.

"All I gotta say, is you have a hell of a lot of nerve."

"Anything for a story, Mr. Warner. Anything for a story."

Chapter 22

WHOOPS

Trevor Doyle had spent a little over three hours in surgery, where the birdshot had been carefully removed from his butt. It was a delicate procedure, a lot like removing splinters.

He opened his eyes, slowly, and blinked a few times until his wife's face came into view. She was seated in a wheelchair beside the bed and flashed him a warm smile.

"Glad you could join us, Daddy Doyle," she greeted. "How's your derriere?"

"Don't ask," he replied, wincing a bit. It felt like he were lying on a bed of pins and needles.

"Curious?"

"Just the facts, ma'am."

She rattled off the highly anticipated information. "Christopher John, 7 lbs. 2 oz., and Michael Alan, 6 lbs. 8 oz. All fingers and toes are present and accounted for."

It took Trevor a few extra seconds, to realize she had just told him they had TWINS. Quite suddenly, his eyes went wide.

"Did you say we have…?" he started.

"Yep. There's two. This day is just full of surprises, isn't it?"

Flipper was chasing the news van but doing so as slowly as he could get away with"" was chasing the news van but doing so as slowly as he could get away with. He thought this whole situation was ludicrous. He was pretty sure the van was headed for Warner's place and hoped when he rounded the corner, it wasn't there.

He spotted the van slipping into the barn and pulled over to give it another minute to "disappear." He saw the barn door being pulled shut and picked up the radio mike.

"Unit 11, here. Anyone listening?"

"Eleven, Travers, here, over."

"I lost 'em up the road somewhere," Flipper lied. "I think they may have gone down the back side of the mountain, over."

He hung up the mike and quickly shut off the radio. Travers would undoubtedly be screaming at him, and he had no intentions of listening to that. He pulled the cruiser into Warner's driveway and parked.

Time to take sides, and he, already, knew which side he wanted to be on.

Jerry grabbed her legs, George underneath her arms. Stephanie Ran down the hall, tothe closet and yanked open the door.

"Hurry up!" she whispered to them.

George and Jerry scurried down to the closet, and unceremoniously heaved Karen inside, with a thud. All three half-dove in with her, shutting the door.

"OOOWWW!!!" screamed the body on the floor. "Get your foot out my crotch!!"

"Shut up, Karen!" Stephanie ordered. "He'll hear us!"

"Remove your foot, whoever you are, or I'll make sure they hear me up in Burlington!"

"What's that smell?" Jerry asked. "It's making me gag."

"Mothballs," George replied from the corner, where he'd crammed himself. "Is that your elbow that keeps hitting me in the ribs?"

"Where's everyone else?" Karen inquired from below. "What happened?"

"Cheryl went for the truck," Jerry whispered, "and, I think, Jake's in the barn. I'm assuming everyone else bolted for the basement."

"This is getting waaaay out of hand," remarked George. "You know, we can't keep this up, much longer."

"What would you rather do, George, eat prison cuisine, or snort mothballs?"

"Neither," he snapped at Jerry.

"Well, those are your ONLY choices, right now," Jerry observed, "until we come up with something, that makes a shred of sense."

"Would someone, please, tell me WHY we're in here, in the first place?" Karen pleaded from below. "I'm getting sick to my stomach."

"Another cruiser was chasing Cheryl," Jerry explained, "He was about a minute behind her. You fainted, so we dragged you in here, out of sight."

"We need to know where he is RIGHT NOW," Stephanie piped up. "I'm gonna poke my head out there, and see what I can find out. For God's sake, DON'T come out 'til I tell ya' to."

Stephanie took a deep breath to steel herself, but only managed to get a noseful of those wretched mothballs, She nearly threw open the closet door, to get out.

"Where'd he go, now, Mr. Warner?"

"Dunno," Jake replied, scanning the driveway, through the crack in the wall.

They had wasted no time, getting up to the hayloft, to hide.

"What do you mean, you don't know?"

"He's gone," Jake announced and sounding confused. "Cruiser is still there, but he must'a gone around back."

"Did anyone remember to lock the door, this time?" Cheryl asked.

She already knew the answer, to that question,

Trevor had listened to Megan relate the events surrounding the jailbreak, and remained quiet for several minutes, after she had finished.

"You know," he finally began, "I'm wishing I hadn't been so pushy about the police department thing. I feel like this mess is all my fault."

"Now, wait one minute, there, mister," Megan said firmly. "NOBODY could've forseen Elsie Warner grabbing a shotgun, and you know it."

Trevor shrugged his shoulders, somewhat unconvinced. "I'm not sure what was the scariest part," he admitted, "her aiming that shotgun at me, or that dress and apron combo, she was wearing." He closed his eyes and shook his head, trying to get that image out of his head. Megan laughed.

"Hey, is my wallet around somewhere?" he asked.

"Right here," she replied, pulling it from her bathrobe's pocket. "There's a little blue slip of paper in there, with a phone number on it. I think it's tucked behind my license." She opened it and, seconds later, she held it up for him to see.

He nodded. "You happen to have your cell?" he asked, fighting back a smile.

Megan just looked at her husband, returning his smile. He was up to something, and she knew it wasn't anything good.

Stephanie had only taken a couple steps towards the kitchen, when the back door started to open. She couldn't run back to the closet, so she ducked into the living room. She, immediately, stumbled into the card table, left there after the morning poker game. She and it went over with a CRASH.

Flipper had just stepped inside when he heard the noise"" had just stepped inside when he heard the noise. Closing the door and engaging the deadbolt, he moved as quickly as he could, towards the sound.

He didn't get far.

Everyone in the basement jumped when they heard the thud upstairs. It was pitch black down there, except for the one flashlight, belonging to Chuck Sanborn. He headed for the stairs, nearly knocking over Warren, on the way. He took the stairs, and seconds later, he was gone.

Flipper never heard anyone come up behind him, so the hand going over his mouth was a complete surprise"" never Flipper" never heard anyone come up behind him, so the hand going over his mouth was a complete surprise. He tried to break free, but he was also being held with an arm around him.

"Knock it off, Flipper, and I'll let ya' go," the voice promised.

Flipper didn't recognize the voice, but only his fellow officers called him by his nickname"" didn'Flipper" didn't recognize the voice, but only his fellow officers called him by his nickname.

"You gonna yell?"

Flipper emphatically shook his head"" emphatically shook his head.

Chuck let go, spun him around, and barked an order. "Move your damn cruiser before someone sees it."

A very clearly, uttered cuss word eminated from the living room.

Stephanie appeared in the doorway. "Too late," she announced.

Petersen pulled in behind "Flipper's" cruiser and parked. He rolled down the window, tossed out his tasteless gum, and lit a cigarette. He looked over at his friend, who was just sitting, there, staring at Warner's house.

"I hope you aren't planning to go in, until we have more help." Dan said. "I know they're not violent, but, it seems our officers have found 'The Bermuda Triangle' of Knicker's Notch. They pull in THIS driveway, and then POOF! They vanish."

Flipper's vehicle was still, here, but he was fairly confident, that it's driver had become another "lost" soul.

Travers didn't respond. He squinted, instead, as if he were focusing in on an image, that only he could see. He removed his glasses, and after wiping them clean with a McDonald's napkin, he replaced them and turned to his friend.

"I'm thinkin', Dan," he said, "now, why don't you radio in and get us a weather update or something?" I need to think some more."

"Well, Mike, don't think too much longer. My vacation starts in sixty-four days. After that, you're on your own."

He switched on the radio and picked up the mike.

Jake and Cheryl left the barn and bolted for the back of the house. Jake was hoping to gain access to the house by using the bulkhead doors. Once they skidded on the wet grass and came to a halt, Cheryl stood watch, while Jake began pounding on the doors. He hoped someone would hear him.

The door to the closet flew open, and Karen fell into the hallway, gagging and choking. If Stephanie wasn't angry before, she certainly was, now.

"MY GOD, KAREN, WHAT'S WRONG WITH YOU?!" she yelled.

"Steph!", Chuck whispered, "Keep your voice down." "WHY?" she shrieked, turning back to face him.

Flipper side-stepped to the right quickly"" siFlipper" side-stepped to the right quickly. He was NOT going to be in

the middle of whatever it was that was coming.

"Does it REALLY matter any more?" she nearly screamed. She pointed her thumb over her shoulder. "No matter what we do," Jumpy Jordan here is gonna screw it up!"

Chuck leaned to the left of Stephanie, to see Karen sprawled on the floor and gasping for air, like a fish out of water.

"Hey, Karen," he called to her, "Get a grip, will ya? We got enough problems and you're not helping."

George had just stepped out of the closet, and his eyes nearly popped out of his head. He had only heard THAT particular phrase once before, and he never, really, expected to hear it again. Especially coming from a female, and never from a female state trooper. "I love you, too," Chuck answered her.

Cheryl could see that Jake's pounding was going unheard. It was no competition for the thunder and pouring rain. They needed to get inside and out of sight, fast. She shoved Jake aside, and using the flat side of an ax handle, she'd just found, she began slamming it against the metal door, with a vengeance. The bulkhead door flew open on the 5th try, and if Mike Cummings wasn't paying attention, he would've gotten a piece of the 6"

Cheryl grabbed Jake and practically pushed him down the steps, into the depths of the basement.

Dan switched off the radio and shook his head.

"That's weird," he observed. "I'm not getting anything at all on the radio, Mike. Nothing."

"Must be the weather," Travers guessed. "The wind and rain are messing with the signals. Try your cell."

Dan dug it out, flipped it open, and swore.

"No signal on mine. Got yours?"

Travers dug his out and handed it over. Dan took it and checked the screen.

"There's a signal, but it's a really weak one," he announced, doubting that would do them much good. "Who shall we call?"

"I heard that a text message will go through, even when a call won't," Travers said. "Give that a shot. Send it to Sandy. She's ALWAYS got her phone on and will get it instantly."

Sandy was Traver's long-time girlfriend, and a 3rd grade teacher.

They had met six years ago, when he had gone to the school to do a class on safety. Thankfully, she not only liked Dan, his best friend, but had grown close to his girlfriend, Kim. The foursome spent a lot of time together.

"Will do," Dan agreed. "Hope this goes through."

He began to type, while Travers returned to his thoughts.

Megan opened the cell, dialed the number on the paper, and handed the phone to her husband.

"Are you gonna tell me what you're up to?" she asked, watching as he checked the screen and then, hit SEND.

He help up a finger, signaling she needed to wait. He flashed her a huge smile when the phone began to ring.

"I'm just checking to see if anyone's home," he replied, "but, mostly, I want to know if anyone is dumb enough to answer."

Everyone was upstairs now, and just about everyone, was arguing. It started in the basement. Jake was furious, when he discovered that he had stepped in shit in the barn. Elsie made some remark about how he'd "better not track it through the house."

Jake responded to that, by marching right past his spouse and up the stairs. Elsie followed, scolding him all the way, and everyone else chose to follow.

Now, they were spread out—some in the kitchen, some in the living room, and some in the hall. The bickering was growing louder by the minute.

Trooper Karen Jordan had retreated to the bathroom, to splash cold water on her face. After wiping her face with a towel, she decided to take a look out the window.

That was strange. Travers was still sitting there, and by her calculations, he'd been there over ten minutes. It didn't make any sense. He should've been pounding on the door, or shouting threats through a bullhorn.

She turned her attention to the growing noise and left the bathroom.

Jake's phone began to ring, which brought a modicum of silence to the group. Elsie, who was standing right next to it, snatched it up and politely greeted the caller.

"Hello?"

Jake slapped his forehead with the palm of his hand, and Elsie waved him off with a "don't bother me" look. It took about seven more seconds to register, and when she realized what she'd done, she slammed the receiver back into it's cradle.

She looked around the darkened room, noting the horrified look on everyone's faces. She shrugged and looked over at Jake.

"Whoops."

Trevor was holding the phone out in front of him, staring at it, as if were last night's winning lottery ticket.

"I can't believe someone actually answered," he declared, in disbelief. "You sure, it was Warner's number?" Megan asked, "maybe you should be sure."

Trevor pushed a couple buttons, to locate the phone's call history. He read off the numbers, which Megan verified were the same ones on the slip of blue. paper.

"How did you know, they'd be at Jake and Elsie's?" Megan asked, sliding the paper back into Jake's wallet. "I would think, that would be the LAST place they would go. It's the FIRST place the cops would look, don't you think?"

"If Jake is running this circus," Trevor replied, "he'd want to be on his home turf. He can't very well tell the others what to do if he's hiding out in someone else's house." "Poor Elsie," Megan remarked, with a tiny smile. "She's probably being strung from a beam in the basement by the angry mob for that mistake."

"Yeah," Trevor agreed, with a bigger smile, "still raining too hard, to burn her at the stake, in the town square..."

They looked at each other, attempting to treat the matter, as seriously as possible

They burst out laughing.

Petersen had changed the content of the text message several times, in an effort to be clear and thorough. Once he was satisfied, he turned to Travers who sat, there, now, with his eyes closed.

"Ok, Mike, how's this sound?"

Travers opened his eyes and turned to Petersen. The expression on his face made it very clear he was very irritated at being bothered.

He grunted to signal, that he was listening.

"Mike and Dan at KN. Unable to reach dispatch via radio. One phone, no signal.

One phone, very weak. Need storm update and HELP ASAP. Reply via text ONLY."

"Fine. Send it," was all Travers managed, going back to his own thoughts.

(and planet, thought Dan)

Petersen double-checked the phone number for Sandy, then opted to add two more: Kim and his sister. The more people who got the message, the better the odds, someone would get it and respond.

He was about to push the SEND button, when he decided to add three more words: WE LOVE YOU. Off into the stormy stormyair, it went.

Things had come to a screeching halt, when Elsie hung up the phone.

No one moved. No one coughed or even sneezed. It wasn't until she uttered that one word, that everyone began to argue with one another. The word "whoops" had the same effect, as the opening bell of a boxing match.

Elsie was stunned, and overwhelmed, too, with guilt. Her recklessness had caused all this, and got all her neighbors in trouble. These were her friends, who were, now, at each other's throats.

Andy and John were facing off, with Andy being the first to start the feud.

"Hey," he'd snapped, "I've been meaning to ask you where the hell is my sip'sow?" John couldn't believe what he was hearing.

"Oh, for God's sake, Andy," John shot back, "everyone here is on the FBI's "Most Wanted" list, and you're worried about your rusty jigsaw?" Are you kidding me?"

"I just remembered," he replied, "so I'm asking, and it better NOT be rusty, because it was fine when I lent it to you."

"Are you tryin' to…" John started, but George suddenly pushed his way in between them.

"STOP IT!" George yelled, looking from one to the other. "Just stop. If you can't play nice, get out'a the sandbox."

"Hey, John," came another voice, from behind him. It was Warren, who tapped him on the shoulder to get his at-tion. "Did you figure out what to do about Abner?"

John spun around so fast, Warren actually jumped back foot or so. "What about Abner?"

"I was wondering if you knew what you were going to do," Warren explained. "You know, how you'll get him back?"

"Back from where?" he snapped, taking Warren by the collar. "Back from where? WHERE is he?"

George stepped in and separated the two, then turned to John "Calm down," he ordered, "It's not his fault. We thought you had been told about it." George himself, now, took a step back. He knew what John's reaction was going to be, and wanted to be clear of it.

"The State cops took him to the pound," he finally, said.

Chapter 23

FREEING A FRIEND

George saw the blood drain out of John's face in a split second, and when his eyes widened, he backed up so fast he bumped into Andy.

John said nothing. Instead, as if someone had flipped a switch, he barreled his way through everyone like an NFL linebacker, with seconds left to reach the END ZONE. He also had the same results. George got shoved into Marlene, who stumbled into Jake. Chuck Sanborn, who was consulting with "Flipper," found himself crashing forward into him, taking them both to the floor. Just like in the game, there was a lot of grunting and cussing as John made his way to the kitchen and the back door. George yelled after him to STOP! But John had one thing on his mind.

Springing the furball.

Jake spun around and glared at George.

"Now what?" he demanded. "What in hell did you say to him, and where is he goin'?"

George gave his wife a desperate look, afraid to answer. He just created another problem, and he knew he should've just kept his trap shut.

"WELL?!" Jake nearly yelled, taking a step towards George.

George mumbled.

"GEORGE!" Marlene snapped at her husband. "What did you say?"

"I told him about Abner," he admitted finally.

Jake ran a hand thru his unkempt hair, then wandered over to the Lazy-Boy in the corner. No one said a word, watching him as he, carefully, lowered himself into it.

Jake sat there, quietly, for nearly a minute, then he raised his head. He opened and closed his eyes a couple of times, then peered out at them over the rim of his glasses. "Else?"

"Yes, dear?" she answered softly from the corner of the room. She was certain he was going to start yelling at her for answering the phone. She moved around Karen and Stephanie, where he could see her in the dim light. "What is it?" she asked.

"Get my pipe," he said, flatly.

Peterson was moving up the driveway as slowly as he could. Travers had pulled out a pair of binoculars and was searching the upstairs windows for any signs of life. It wasn't easy, with the rain coming down so hard.

"This is nothin' but a waste of time," Travers complained. "They could be gettin' by us right now."

"I know, Mike," Dan conceded, "but Doyle insisted we check his shed for them, said it would be a perfect place for them to hide." "Well, I don't agree," Mike snapped, tossing the binoculars into the backseat. They bounced off the back and landed on the floor with a "thud."

"We need to get back to Warner's," he added, ignoring the sound.

"Alright, alright," Dan said, "we'll drive around back to the shed and then go. He said, There's plenty of room to turn around."

"Fine," Travers barked. "But, if we lose them 'cause of this "goose chase"..."

Dan didn't need to hear the rest of it. He continued on around the back of the house, where the shed sat, directly ahead at the end of the drive. Seeing the big puddle, which was about the length and width of the cruiser, made him smile. It reminded him of the one that used to appear in front of his grandparents' house as a kid. He and his brother would get out their trucks and boats and pretend it was a carwash. He couldn't help but step on the gas a bit and plow his way through it.

He chuckled, and Travers swore.

He had good reason to.

Karen spun around and shoved Stephanie aside, nearly knocking over a floor lamp. She ran for the bathroom to see where John was headed and if Travers would see him. Pete and Linda, who hadn't said much until now, agreed they needed to sit down. They plopped themselves down on the couch and began to whisper to each other.

"I think we should just turn ourselves in," came a voice from the corner.

Marge Burroughs made her way through the group until she was standing in front of Jake. Her husband had been hiding behind Chuck, in the shadows, content with someone else running this circus. He joined his wife and squeezed her hand in support.

"I agree, Jake," he said hesitantly. "I think..."

"Go get him," Jake cut him off.

"Get who? What?"

"John!" Jake yelled. "Go get him 'fore he does something unfixable!"

Burr mumbled something no one could hear. Correction. ALMOST no one. Marge heard him, and her thoughts raced to the scratches on her face and how they got there.

"Go get 'em yerself, you self-righteous..."

"Uh oh," Marge said.

Trevor was laughing so hard, Megan thought, Sure, he'd pop a stitch. He'd pulled a pillow from behind his head, and was, now, clutching it to his stomach as he sat up in bed. Megan was nearly doubled-over in the wheelchair, laughing, too. Neither one had laughed that hard since Trevor had put too much detergent in the washer.

They'd been laughing so loudly, a nurse had poked her head in, to check on them. Seeing there was no need to interrupt, she'd left wondering what was so funny. A couple more minutes passed before Megan wiped her eyes and took a deep breath.

"Ok, Hon," she said, "I get why you sent them to check on our place. I don't get. Why you didn't call Warner's and tell them to run for it?" Trevor ran a hand through his matted hair, turned to his wife, and smiled.

"It's not necessary," he replied simply.

"Why not?" she asked. "They won't find anyone at our house and go back. What's the point?"

"Do you remember the first day we saw the house?"

"Of course, I do. I was three months pregnant and sick as a dog. Why?"

"Anything else about that day, that sticks out in your mind?"

Megan's blue eyes narrowed and focused in on the memory. A moment passed before she shook her head.

"Walk us through the visit," Trevor suggested.

"Ok, ok," she agreed, "let's see..."

She spent the next few minutes talking about the house. She talked about the big kitchen, the bedrooms, and the room she chose for an office. She finished by mentioning the enormous weeping willow tree on the front lawn.

Trevor sighed.

"When we got done touring the house," he said, "what did we do next?"

Megan scrunched up her eyebrows and bit her lower lip. She was growing a bit frustrated, having no idea where he was going with all this.

"We told the realtor to send us the paperwork; we wanted it, all that stuff," she responded, "then we left."

Trevor shook his head.

Megan's mouth opened wide enough to toss a baseball in. "Huh?"

"What kind of day was it?"

"Awful," she said flatly, "wet and windy, like today."

"Remember what happened out back?"

"Oh God, yeah, oh boy, did we get stuck in all that mud. Had to call a tow

to pull us out, and..."

Megan finally got the picture.

Someone was screaming.

The floor lamp went over, this time, and Stephanie went with it. It was close enough to the window so that the very top went right into it. CRASH.

It was Elsie, who was doing the screaming, furious that someone had broken her reading lamp. She didn't even give the window a second thought.

"ELSIE, SHUT UP!" Marlene shrieked, stunning everyone. Even Warren was shocked, not having heard her yell like that in all their years of marriage. Generally, she was very slow to raise her voice for any reason. "It's just an old lamp, you fool!!"

Marlene had been standing there, waiting to see Jake's reaction to what Burroughs had just said to him. Elsie had plowed through the group and screamed right in her ear. Elsie, now, spun around to face Marlene, her face beet-red with anger.

"It may be an old lamp, honey," she spat at her, "but it was MY lamp, in My house, and YOURE TRESPASSIN!!"

Marlene took a step closer, so their noses were just inches apart.

"Did you say 'trespassing?" she asked. "We're sure not here for the barbecue." Elsie started to respond, but Marlene was far from being finished.

"YOU got us all into this," she went on, "and you haven't even offered us all a post-incarceration cocktail!"

The only thing that kept Elsie from slapping Marlene was the groaning coming from Stephanie. She had propped herself up against the wall.

"I need some ice," she mumbled.

Elsie turned on her now.

"HOW did you ever get to be a police person?" she asked with sarcasm-soaked words,

"Win the church raffle, did ya?"

"Leave her alone," Marge said, from behind Marlene.

"Oh for..." Elsie sputtered, turning back to she and Marlene, "She's askin' for ice when there isn't any power! HOW can she be tellin' the cops what to do on the radio, when she's Dumb enough to screw up a two-cor funeral??"

The sound of Marlene's hand connecting with Elsie's cheek sounded just like a ball splitting a bat,

The room descended into chaos..

Travers opened the car door, struggling against the wind and rain. He took his nightstick and drove it straight down into the mud until it hit solid ground. Dan watched in silence as he pulled it back out and inspected it, like one testing a pan of brownies. He said nothing as he closed the door and tossed it into the backseat.

Dan removed his hat and rubbed his chin, waiting for his friend to speak. Travers, however, just sat there, staring straight ahead.

"Mike, I.."

"Don't."

"I didn't..."

"Don't..."

"Are you gonna...?"

"Call a tow…" was all Travers could say.

"We can't, Dan responded softly."Phones are dead, and Dispatch is off the air, remember?"

"TRY," he ordered.

CHAPTER 24

FLYING LESSONS

The man behind the counter was chewing on his pencil, studying the paper in front of him, stopping occasionally to make notes. He heard someone pull into the parking lot but ignored it. More often than not, it was someone turning around because they missed the road just before it. It was unmarked and hard to spot at night.

He glanced at the wall clock and realized it was closing time. He needed to do his rounds quickly if he wanted to make it to the sports bar to place his bets. He set down his notes and headed for the door that led out to the back. He chose not to turn the lights on out there, preferring to go by the one soft bulb at the far end of the room.

This was Jericho's "no-kill" animal shelter, and Martin Cooper, age 62, was more than just the guy on the night shift. He owned it 34 years ago, just after he and his wife, Helen, married, they discovered a box of new puppies abandoned at the local laundromat. They raised them and found them good homes, keeping one for themselves, of course. They were surprised to find the nearest shelter was over in Burlington, and a year later, they opened this one.

Through the years, the shelter had housed all kinds of animals, not just dogs and cats. They would never turn away any animal in need of help, and although the shelter could house around 25, it rarely passed a dozen.

Tonight, there were only eleven, and all seemed to be content at the moment. They had all been fed, watered, and played with, and now, some were, actually, snoring. He walked the length of the cages, acknowledging wagging tails by name.

"Hey, Snickers," he called to the Boxer on his right. He was slow to wander over, but once he got to the cage door, Martin reached in and scratched his head. He moved on, where Bazooka, a 6-year-old beagle, waited for the same attention.

Martin made his way down to the last cage on his left. He stood there, hands on his hips, and eyeballed his newest tenant. BIG was the first word that came to mind, but not at all intimidating. He had been brought in earlier in the day by two state troopers. Once he'd been placed in the oversized pen, he ate his weight in kibble and drank a bathtub's worth of water. Now, he lay there, returning Martin's questioning gaze. "You OK, Abner?" Martin asked. "I'm headed home and wanted to be sure you're alright."

Abner merely tilted his head to the side.

"I'm sure you'll be out in no time," he said with enthusiasm. "He sure will," came a voice by the door. Abner barked.

Martin turned to face the voice, and although it was dim light, he saw something he didn't like at all.

Dan replaced the radio mike and waited. Travers sat there, staring at a windshield that couldn't be seen through.

"Mike?"

"Shut it, Dan, I'm thinking."

"Mike, listen...."

"I SAID."

"NO! You shut up!" Dan barked.

Mike was stunned, but not because of Dan's insubordination, but, rather, because of his tone.

He and Dan rarely argued.

"Look, I get it, Mike," Dan explained, lowering his voice, "You want 'em and we'll get 'em, but we can't do any more in this storm. Even if we weren't stuck, it's getting dangerous. You heard the forecast, high winds and all that. Trees are starting to come down. We need to get out of this cruiser and into shelter."

"Can't get in here," Mike finally conceded. "I'm sure he's got an alarm, and I'm not getting into that sort of mess."

They sat in silence for a couple of minutes before Mike spoke again.

"Let's check out the barn."

"The barn?" Dan asked, astonished. "That ain't safe!"

"I'm not looking to take shelter in it," Mike explained, exasperated. "I want to see what's IN it."

Dan followed his finger as it pointed to the old, grey structure. "Doyle's got a 4X4 AND a Harley," Mike went on, "I'm willing to bet he's got something else we can use in there."

Dan cracked a smile for the first time in hours.

"Look, mister," Martin said, holding up his hands, "I don't want any trouble."

"Snickers" and "Sergio," a Collie, began to growl.

"You won't get any." John told him. "So long as I can take my dog there."

Abner barked twice, this time barely able to control his joy at seeing his master. He started running circles around the cage in anticipation.

Martin looked over at Abner, then back to the figure in the doorway, who was balancing a 30-30 shotgun on his arm.

"Look, Mister," he spoke cautiously, "I'm not in the business of dog-napping, so you don't need to be barreling in like the Marines, springing a hostage."

"Yeah, I do," John countered. "State Police took him, and I've come to get him. I don't want to use this, but if I have to, I'll start with the windows". Just show me some ID, Martin said, "then all you have to do is sign for him."

John Melbourne rubbed the stubble on his chin, giving that some thought. He set the shotgun down and leaned against the doorway.

"Can't prove he's mine," he admitted. "Got him over in Burlington from a friend about six years ago. Named him Abner after my great-grandpa."

Martin had no doubt it was his. Who else brings a shotgun to a shelter unless they're hell-bent on getting their best friend? Abner barked again, as if to strengthen his conclusion.

"Take the shotgun back to your vehicle first," Martin said, "then come back and get your buddy. I just don't want that thing in here. Fair enough?"

John turned and left.

Martin turned to Abner and smiled at him. "Well, Ab, you're going home."

"Why go there?" Dan was asking, buttoning his rain slicker and securing the hat on his head with the chin strap. It was pointless, really, as they'd taken several minutes to traverse the mud to get to the barn. They were as drenched as any human could possibly get.

"I've been up there," Mike answered, mimicking his friend's preparations. "There's a set of bulkhead doors that lead into the cellar, and if we're lucky, they're unlocked."

"No one's up there, I don't think," Dan said, so we can always break in. " "I'd rather not," Mike replied, "but if we're REALLY lucky, when the storm winds down, they may show up." Dan dropped his smoke and stamped it out in the dirt. He didn't want to burn down Doyle's barn.

They were already stealing his ATV.

The living room was never meant to hold so many people. Certainly not so many. pushing, shoving, and clawing at each other.

Elsie took Marlene to the floor seconds after she'd been slapped. Marge Burroughs had left her husband's side to help Karen pull them apart. They hadn't succeeded, as now all four were rolling around on the floor, cussing and yelling.

Jake was busy yelling at Burroughs, who was taking Jake so seriously, he was unaware his wife was getting her hair pulled out.

George and Warren stood in shock for a few seconds before finally deciding to try and split up Jake and Burroughs. Stephanie had managed to dodge the bodies, and she now entered the kitchen to find Chuck, Jerry, Cheryl, and "Flipper." Cheryl gasped when she saw the bump forming rapidly on Stephanie's forehead. "Jeeze, Steph," Jerry observed, "are you OK? Want some ice or…"

He stopped, hoping no one would make a smart remark about the power, like Elsie had to Marlene.

Cheryl took her and guided her, carefully, to a chair at the table. Flipper, who had had a crush on her since forever, seized the opportunity to show his affection, He moved his chair closer, took her hand in his, and then rubbed her back with the other.

"Thanks, Terri," she said softly, using his real name. "I'm OK, really. Just a bump on my brick-hard head."

"Flipper" knew how she felt. He'd swerved to avoid a turtle three years ago, which resulted in him losing control and flipping the vehicle. Thus, his nickname was born.

Chuck looked around at the tired faces before him, all looking to him for an idea he didn't have.

"Can someone go get Karen?" he asked.

"She's responding to a fight call in the living room," Cheryl remarked.

It was amusing, but no one laughed. They needed to stop the endless bickering and physical confrontations, or someone was going to get hurt, BADLY.

"Let's get everyone together to figure things out," Jerry suggested. "We need a plan of action before the storm ends. Agreed?"

Everyone nodded, and one by one, they began to leave the kitchen.

It took Dan and Mike several minutes to get to Warner's house. The wind was whipping in all directions, and visibility was terrible. Limbs had come down; they had to move or avoid them, and there was a river of debris they had to drive on.

Mike was hanging on with one hand, a shotgun tightly gripped in the other.

Dan had stopped caring. He drove across Jake's lawn, crossed the driveway, and roared around the back of the house. He took the corner too fast and saw the tree root too late.

Mike went airborne.

It was a stroke of luck (or an outright miracle) that Stephanie didn't get hurt.

She had just bent to tie her shoe when the window shattered, coinciding with a loud "boom" outside. Everyone dove for cover, while someone screamed, "We're all gonna die!"

"Jerry, who the hell is shooting at us?" Stephanie asked.

He crawled to the sink, stood, and peered out into the yard. He blinked several times, trying to reconcile with his tired brain what he was seeing. He observed a few seconds more, then turned and sat on the floor.

"Well?" She pushed.

Jerry was horrified to see the hole in the wall, right behind where Stephanie had been sitting.

"Two troopers," he finally told her, "But I don't think it was on purpose. One looks like he got thrown because the other is hovering over him."

Cheryl and Chuck crawled back into the kitchen.

"NOW WHAT?" Cheryl asked.

"Should we go for the basement, or what?" Stephanie asked.

Somebody had to make a decision now; their planned discussion would have to wait.

"Must be Travers and Peterson," Chuck observed. "They're the only ones who are dumb enough to be out here still. Keep an eye on 'em. I'll tell everyone what's going on."

Jerry nodded as Chuck left the kitchen. Standing up, he turned to look outside when something suddenly slammed in the basement.

"Uh-oh," he announced, "We got company."

"Take it easy, Mike," Dan said to his friend. "You took quite a hit when you hit the ground."

"How the hell would you know?" Mike snapped. "You took that corner so fast, you didn't even know you lost me! What did you hit, anyway?"

"Tree root," Dan answered. "Damn big one, too." Almost lost control of "Well, ya' sure lost me," Mike grimaced, lowering himself to sit on the step.

Dan found a folding chair and sat down. He removed his hat, unbuttoned his slicker, and dug out a handkerchief to wipe his face. He looked at Mike and could see, clearly, he was in pain. He glanced around the dark cellar while drops of rain fell to the floor, creating tiny puddles.

"I think I might've busted a rib or two," Mike admitted, touching his right side. "Haven't felt like this since my days at the academy."

Mike looked up at his friend and noticed a strange look on his face.

"What?" he asked.

"Look around you, Mike, and tell me what you see."

Jake knew full well what the noise in the cellar meant and wasted no time in getting to the kitchen. He passed the word to everyone in the living room, which brought the ladies' brawl to an abrupt halt. It was eerie. The wind and rain outside were relentless, yet the silence indoors seemed almost deafening.

Jake walked in and scanned the faces. He didn't seem to notice the hole in the wall.

"Mr. Warner," Chuck whispered, "Travers and his buddy are in the basement." "I know," he replied. "I've lived in this house for fifty years. I know what those bulkhead doors sound like."

"Flipper" did what no one had the presence of mind to do. He went over to the cellar door and, very carefully, engaged the deadbolt.

He sat back down and noticed all eyes were on him.

"Seemed like a good idea," he said, smiling, "and, now, we have 'em where we want 'em."

"Not quite," Jake stated. "They can get out the same way they got in."

Stephanie swore. "What can we do?"

Everyone looked at each other, waiting for the answer to come from someone other than themselves. The storm outside had intensified in the last couple of hours, which didn't leave them with any viable options. It was Jake who broke the silence first, heading for the door.

"I'm going out to the barn," he announced. "Find something to secure those bulkhead doors with. Anyone care to help?"

Jerry went to get his jacket.

"That's great," Cheryl observed, "But, once the animals are in their cage, then what? When they realize we're up here and they're locked in down there..."

Stephanie burst out laughing, then tried to stifle the sound of it. She laughed and laughed for nearly three minutes before she stopped long enough to utter three words: "I got it." She laughed for another couple of minutes before she wiped her eyes, took a deep breath, and let them in on the fun.

Travers still didn't have a clue what Dan saw that he didn't.

"Look, Buddy," he said, "I'm tired, wet, hungry, and hurtin', thanks to your professional driving skills. You need to tell me what you're lookin'..."

There was a thud, followed by a scraping sound on the bulkhead doors. They exchanged confused looks.

"That did NOT sound good, at all," Dan muttered as he jumped up and headed towards them.

He pushed on the right-side door, which gave way about four inches before it stopped. He saw the chain and froze for a moment. He dropped his hands to his sides and cursed himself for calling Mike with the "tip" that led them here. Now, in a cruel twist of fate, they were locked up, NOT THEM. A moment passed, and he found himself smiling as he turned to his friend.

"Well, Dan, what was it?"

The door at the top of the stairs suddenly closed, which got Travers up and taking them at light speed. It was dark up there, but he could still see what had been left on the top step.

A jar of peanut butter, a loaf of bread, a knife, napkins, and two six-packs of beer.

Mike didn't bother trying the door.

Trevor hung up the phone, took a sip of his coffee, and then dialed the number for his wife's room.

"Hi, Papa Doyle," she greeted cheerfully. "How's your butt?"

"Sure," he admitted, smiling. "If you're not busy, I would love to see your adorable face."

"Something wrong?"

"No," he replied, "but if you've recovered from the last fit of laughter, I have news that' split your stitches."

"I'll bring a pillow," she told him, and hung up.

Trevor dug out the number for Stephen Drewer and dialed.

"THEY DID WHAT?!" Judge Willis yelled into the phone.

He swung his legs out of bed and sat up, glancing at the clock, 10:08pm. Not as late as he thought.

"Uncle, calm down and listen, please," Stephen asked, wincing at being screamed at.

"I've got a better idea," Willis told him. "Get on your rain gear and get over here. I gotta hear this in person."

He hung up the phone and reached for his robe.

"I'm gonna buy Jake Warner a beer when this is over," he mumbled. "Hell, I'll buy the brewery if he pulls this off."

The news van came to an abrupt halt, for the fifth time, in less than a mile.

"OK, guys!" Jerry called out, from the driver's seat, "Got another one!" The back doors flew open, and out jumped Flipper, Chuck, and Burroughs, who'd been the first to volunteer for the "debris removal teams." There were three, altogether, and it made it easier on everyone to divide up the work. "Team Burroughs darted around to the front of the van, and in no time flat hauled the large oak limb out of the way."

They had decided to go down the back side of the mountain, assuming that the bridge was out by now. It was dark, and the storm had raged on, unabated. It wasn't just dangerous to be out in this weather but downright stupid. No one, however, had seemed to care when Stephanie laid out her plan.

They were in this together, and even though they'd done some arguing and all that, it was to be expected under such circumstances.

Many of these folks had known each other for years. In some cases, all their lives. The Warners, Corbetts, Mitchells, and Burroughs had met one year while camping in New Hampshire. The following year, they chose Castleback Mt. for their getaway and fell in love with it instantly.

They were young, but they wanted to make this place their home and set out to do just that. They contacted the state and were granted permission to build, provided they adhered to strict regulations. They were willing to do whatever it took to make this a home where they could live quietly, raise their kids, and pursue those things they loved, such as farming, gardening, fishing, hunting, etc.

The store was built shortly after they settled in, and they had been on the mountain eight years when they decided they needed a post office. Burroughs and George worked in Jericho and Burlington, respectively, and had been picking up the mail. It was becoming a problem, as neither one often got out of work before the post office closed, and days would pass without anyone getting mail. One afternoon, they were all in front of the store discussing it.

Warren had gone and gotten the forms to submit, but they had a problem.

Their "town" had no name.

The discussion had gone on for over two hours, with all kinds of suggestions, but no one seemed to agree on any of them.

"Come on, you guys," Warren pleaded, "this is ridiculous. All we need is a name, and we can be done with it. I've got things to do and can't stand here, all...".

"Don't get your knickers in a twist, Warr," Jake snapped.

"That's it!" Marlene shouted, startling everyone.

Everyone just looked at her, waiting for her to share her sudden revelation.

Five minutes later, "Knickers Notch" was born and officially established in 1958.

They'd been through a lot together, and if they stuck together, they'd get through this, too.

CHAPTER 25

ROUND 3 (WAS IT 4?)

"Are they out of their minds?" Megan asked, "I mean, have they thought this through?"

Trevor had considered the plan, looking at it from all the angles he could come up with, so he didn't hesitate to answer.

"If the right people do the right things, they should get away with it."

"Yeah," she agreed, "but will they?"

"I think so," he replied, with a hint of hesitation. "Everyone in Vermont knows what's going on up on that mountain. If people are taking sides, it's a sure bet THEY'RE RE rootin', for the wrong side of the law."

Megan shook her head in disbelief, trying to figure out how things got so out of control so fast. A simple accident had turned into a manhunt for a bunch of older folks. Megan looked at her husband. She knew the answer to the question she was about to ask, but she needed to hear the answer nonetheless.

"Are you gonna...?"

"Absolutely NOT," he stated firmly, "and if someone had taken the time to ask me that question 36 hours ago, we wouldn't be having this conversation in the first place. Megan saw his face turn red, a sign of anger he rarely displayed.

"NO ONE asked," he repeated. "And, now, those poor folks are out, in this dangerous weather, trying to prove something." THEIR INNOCENCE, she offered.

"That, and they're good people who would never hurt another soul."

Judge Willis was nearly finished with his second cup of Irish coffee, this one being twice as strong as the first.

Stephen had spent twenty minutes, or so, explaining what Doyle had told him. He watched his uncle's face, searching for any signs that the man was about to blow a spark plug or two.

"Who called Doyle?" he inquired, re-lighting his cigar.

"Stephanie Wilson," he answered, "the same one who slugged Travers and got the gang out in the first place. I have to be honest, Uncle. I really think her idea may work, and under the circumstances, we need to try."

"Who do we call, over at the station, to set this in motion?" Willis asked through a thick cloud of stogie smoke. Stephen could tell this was an El Cheapo, not an El Producto, by the smell of it. The man had more money than the state treasury, but he still insisted on buying the cheap stuff. He waved away the cloud bank before answering.

"Doyle and Stephanie are handling those details."

"So, we wait?"

"We wait."

"Jerry?" Warner asked, leaning closer so the man could hear him. The wind and rain were making a lot of noise outside. "You want me to drive this dumpster awhile? I've driven trucks like this in bad weather, so I can help."

"No thanks," Jake, Jerry replied, downshifting. Every leaf, on every tree, in the county had blown off and landed on this road. So it seemed. It made for very hazardous and slippery driving.

Jerry managed a quick look over at Jake and realized he had accumulated a lot of respect for the man. The man was stubborn and liked to do things his way, but he had a loyalty to his wife and friends that was immeasurable and unshakable.

"Hey, Jake," Jerry said, with a friendly tone. "Yes, sir?"

"Don't call me 'sir," Jerry scolded. "If you crack that window some, you're welcome to have a tug or two on your pipe."

Jerry couldn't see Jake's face, but he could almost "hear" the smile erupting on it.

Mike and Dan heard everyone leave. They made no attempt to be quiet, when they did so, sounding like a herd of cattle at a round-up.

They didn't bother to try and gain their freedom. They knew their threats would be ignored and, more likely, laughed at. They chose, instead, to focus on their situation in the tiny, cluttered basement.

They rummaged around for a while, finding dry clothes, towels, and several blankets. It became obvious to them that at some point, they, too, had been in the basement because of the items that were left lying around. One of those items was a Coleman lantern holding a full well of kerosene.

They said nothing to one another as they searched the bags and boxes. It wasn't an issue of being angry with each other but, rather, a shared sense of total humiliation at winding up here. There was a marked difference between how each was handling the hand Fate dealt them. Dan knew, and accepted, that they had been outsmarted.

He knew Mike, on the other hand, was furious, and if it were physically possible, he'd have flames shooting from his nostrils and smoke pouring from his ears. He and Mike had known each other since high school, so he was acutely aware of how Mike handled everything—from bad news to bad food. He'd seen him yelling and seen him enjoying the silence as he worked on a major problem.

He'd spent the last hour observing Mike's actions, looking for something that might betray his thoughts and give him a clue what was coming. He'd paid very close attention, and much to his surprise, he saw nothing.

Mike took a chair and opened a beer.

"Warm, but well-deserved," he announced, handing one to his friend. "Not much else to do but sit here, get drunk, and sing campfire songs."

Dan opened his can and sipped slowly. Mike studied his friend for a minute before leaning back and lighting a cigarette. "What's the problem, Dan? Other than these wonderful accommodations?"

"Don't be a wise-ass," Dan shot back. "I can see through your charade. You're furious and planning something; I just don't know what."

Mike inhaled on his Marlboro deeply, gulped the rest of his beer, and then reached for another.

"Don't worry," Mike told him, "All you have to do is drive. Preferably, without getting me killed, that is."

Cheryl held up her phone. if she could finally get a signal. She had plugged the charger in back when she parked in the barn, so now it was ready to go. She had sent Stephanie back to get a couple of numbers from Chuck. She made her way along as carefully as she could, and she managed to find Marlene's foot.

"OW!" she screamed. "That was my foot; you just stomped on it! "You got two of 'em, old girl, so get over it!" Elsie shot at her.

"You wouldn't be saying that if it were YOUR foot! Marlene snapped at her. It was painfully obvious that the living room brawl was NOT over; rather, it had taken a brief hiatus, and that appeared to be coming to an abrupt end". This van was never meant to hold so many people, Mariere observed. not one's YOUR size Elsie snorted, "Especially not one's VO." Oh no. Marge mumbled," "Here we go.

Jack walked in the front door, greeting fellow officers, who headed He didn't envy them tonight, having to answer all the calls in such nasty weather. He poked his head into the radio room, looking for whoever was at Stephanie's post. He was delighted to see his friend, Liz Palmer, from She had been on maternity leave for the past academy months, but she occasionally filled in at times like this. Lis looked up from her desk, and seeing Jock in the doorway, she jumped up and said to him, "HAAAAAAY, Jack," she greeted him. "I have missed

"They embraced, but it wasn't easy. You know that?" carrying twins, who showed promise of being linebackers for UVT.

"I'm glad to have you here tonight," Jack conceded. "Things are, like, 100 crazy around here."

"I'll bet," Liz observed. "I don't know the whole story, but, I recall, you aren't supposed to be here…"

"SSSSH"

"Don't shush me, Jack," she countered. "I want to know what's going on so I can be prepared for 2 Airborne when they drop in for the rescue."

Jack looked at the duty roster, getting a visual of who was where, and so on. He was happy that he and Liz were the only ones in the building. He just has to convince her to go along. It was either that or getting her to keep her mouth shut.

"OK, OK, hold your water, I'll tell you, but I need you to swear on something near and dear that you're not going to blow any whistles. OK?"

Liz leaned back in the chair, making an attempt to cross her arms across her chest. She was terribly uncomfortable and, looking like a balloon in the Macy's parade, felt very self-conscious.

She eyed Jack carefully, unsure of what to do. They had graduated from the academy together, even going on to work together for the Burlington PD. He got bored with that and decided to become a state trooper, encouraging her to do the same. They were assigned to different stations, but still saw each other often, and the friendship had never wavered.

She had always respected his opinion and knew he had good judgment, so if he was sticking his neck out for these people, that meant something. She made her decision to do the same.

"Alright," she said, finally, "fill me in on this, and don't leave out ONE tiny detail."

Cheryl and Morge overheard the rasty exchange between Elsie and Mariene and wasted no time trying to stop the verbal from going physical. Cheryl got a grip on Marlene's hand, just before it completed its mission, to yank out a chunk of Elsie's silvery grey locks. Marlene's cursing mode is quite clear. That she wasn't happy someone had thwarted her attempt

Marge didn't know what to do but knew she needed to distract Elsie. She took all 138 lbs of herself and threw the equipment case to Elsie. The idea would've worked had Jerry not stopped the van so abruptly. The move didn't just distract Elsie, but the result was Marge's body sliding into Elsie, sending her screaming to the floor.

Trevor held out the phone in front of him, staring at it like it came from outer space. Appropriate, really, considering the call was coming from there (or sounded like it with the fumbling on the other end). He sure felt like he was in it himself. "Who is doing the screaming?" Megan asked, "I bear from here." "Sounds like a fight," Trevor guessed, "a list of groaning and cussing, but. I've no clue who's doing all the fussing and fighting, continued to listen and discern what was going on, up until the connection severed, a minute later "Is that wise?" Megan asked

She never liked to question. Trevor's authority when to police business. She would, gladly, argue over the proper way to hang toilet paper or how much soap was safe to use in order to prevent the dishwasher's "Day of Reckoning," but never ever police business. However, hanging up when people were tearing each other apart on the other end made her nervous.

"I'm not sure," Trevor conceded, "but if that was Stephanie, she's in the middle of it and needs BOTH hands to defend herself from the hair pulling and slapping that undoubtedly is going on."

"Agreed," Megan said. "Did she say where they were?"

"No," he replied, "but something else has me worried."

"We have a pump in our basement for rains like this," he explained. "Yeah, Thank God, we can turn it on when we finally get home. What if Joke hasn't got one?" TREVIA ASKED

Megan stopped smiling.

Elsie did not go to the floor with any grace whatsoever. She didn't go quietly, either. Marlene saw her slide off, turn slightly, and all but land flat on her face.

All who witnessed this burst out into uncontrollable laughter, and this only served to infuriate Elsie further. George helped her off the floor, and she sat back down next to Marge, who looked horrified by what she'd done.

Elsie did the only thing she could think of. She turned, smiled, and shoved Marge. OFF

Jack was waiting for Liz to speak; after giving her the shortest and most detailed version of the story he could. Anything longer would've required visual ads and refreshments during the break.

"What do you do?" Liz asked.

"Whatever you do to keep everyone else away from Atat here," he answered, "even if you have to send 'em out on fake calls."

"We're recorded, remember?" she reminded him.

"Just log them in, as calls made from a cell. As long as there are three or four of them," he told her, "No one's gonna notice."

Liz rolled her eyes, knowing full well she would do it if it came down to that. "Thanks, Liz. I know it's a lot to ask, but these people need a break here. They need your help."

He stood to leave, then added, "Call Steve Drewer; we' need him down here. Call Steve along with the box he removed yesterday."

Liz wanted to ask but decided she didn't want to know.

"Close the door on your way out," she said.

"Why?" Jack asked, confused, "You won't know what's going on."

"THAT'S WHY. If I don't see anything. I won't be lying when I tell them that now, will I?"

Judge Willis hung up the phone and smiled mischievously at his nephew.

"Well?"

"Jack wants you down at the station. Needs your help."

"MY help?" Stephen asked with a high pitch to his voice. "What can I do?"

"Didn't say," Willis answered, "But he did tell you to bring back the box if you still have it."

Stephen was exhausted. It took nearly ten seconds for the words to sink in, like trying to see clearly through a fogged-up windshield. Once his brain cleared and he registered what Jack meant, his jaw dropped. If muscles hadn't anchored his eyeballs, they might have popped right out and hit the far wall.

"What?" Willis asked with his head and hit the far wall.

"No time to explain, uncle," Stephen said, grabbing his rain poncho, "call him back. Tell him I still have what he DIDN'T flush".

Willis started to say something, but Stephen cut him off.

"NOT NOW PLEASE, just call and tell him, precisely, what I just told you." He turned and was gone, leaving Willis standing there with his mouth open.

CHAPTER 26

THE WAITING GAME.

Virgil Parks hung up the phone, looked at his 20-year-old TIMEX with the deep scratch across the face, and groaned. He didn't mind getting called for a tow in the middle of the night. It was an extra $25 after hours and $50 if the cops had called for It was answering calls in nasty weather like this that he dreaded. HATED

He'd been watching an old Alfred Hitchcock film, which he now switched off as he headed down the hall. He was hoping his 22-year-old son, Scott, was still awake, and the light seeping out from under the door, told him he was. He knocked lightly, opening it to find his son lying on the bed with his iPod earbuds on. He flicked the light switch a couple of times to get his attention. Scott sat up to see his father remove the earbuds.

"What's up, Dad?"

"Do you mind goin' with me on a job?" Virgil whispered so as not to wake his wife in the room behind him. "I know it's nasty weather, but I may need some help on this one."

"I'm your man," he responded. He rolled up the iPod and earphones, stuffed them in his rain slicker's pocket, and then slid his size 11 feet into his boots.

He looked up at his dad, once they were laced, holding up two thumbs.

They left.

Megan had rolled her wheelchair to the phone calls. She was looking for snacks, and Trevor pointed her towards the break room. She found a tray and filled it with sandwiches, chips, cookies, two bananas, and bottled water. Tray in lap, she headed back to the room, pausing at the window to the nursery to check on the boys. She was filled with such a warm, tender feeling, seeing them sleeping so peacefully. She hoped they ALWAYS would— throughout their lives—find that peace in their sleep, and she and Trevor would do everything to see that they did. She entered the room to find Trever, head tilted back, eyes closed. He heard her and sat back up in the bed.

"Wow," he said, eyeing her tray. "Where'd you score the loot of this hour?"

"Robbed a room on the fourth floor," she replied, straight-faced. "Gonna arrest me? Can we discuss my crime over a snack first?"

Trevor just smiled at her as she rolled over to him and set the goodies on the table. Megan noticed he had a somewhat somber look on his face, which worried her a great deal. Megan knew he was deeply upset by the events, even though they'd had fits of laughter over it.

He looked at her for a moment before taking a deep breath and speaking.

"I need to be there," he announced, making it clear by his tone that there was no room for discussion on the matter.

"Why?" Megan asked, alarmed at his decision.

"I started this," he explained, pointing to himself with his thumb. "I need to be there to make sure this ends well."

"Honey," Megan protested, "this was NOT your fault or even Elsie's, for that matter. It was an accident. NOTHING MORE. Why not let them handle it? You said, It's a good plan."

"I know you're trying to be supportive," he replied, "and I love you for it, but I've thought a lot about it and made up my mind. I'm going."

Megan found herself, once more, having to defer. This was police business, and he was calling the shots.

"OK, OK," she conceded, "just be careful. You just had surgery. remember?"

Trevor gave her a huge smile.

"Anything I can do to help?" she asked.

"Yup," he answered, "you can go with me."

The news van had stopped to allow one of the teams to disembark for debris removal. The reason they were still sitting there is Jerry had abandoned his seat to help.

Pete and Linda had tried to help Marge off the floor, but she was too stunned to move at all. "What's the matter, Marge?" Elsie asked, words dripping with hostility.

"Need a Snoopy Band-Aid for those scrapes?" Marlene leaned forward and let Elsie have it, cracking her hard enough to knock her back to the floor.

"HOME RUN!!" Someone yelled.

That was, certainly, true. It was the bottom of the 9th, 2 outs, and a tie game, but it was far from being over.

Marlene had just cleared the dugouts.

Virgil had pulled into Jake's driveway and cut the engine. He tapped his son on the shoulder to get his attention. Scott opened his eyes and took in the scenery. and then turned to his father.

"This is it?" he asked, looking to the house, then the barn. No light, driving rain, 2 am. "Lovely weather, Dad," he observed, sarcastically. "Glad you decided to turn this into a father/son road trip. I'm sure we'll bond forever when this is over."

Virgil burst out laughing, and Scott quickly joined in. Scott seemed to have inherited his sense of humor. He may have been born screaming, but he'd been laughing ever since.

They stopped laughing, after a fashion, and Virgil started to give out the orders.

"Behind that barn, there are two cruisers," he told his son. "The keys are in this Just go out there, start 'em up, and make sure they're running OK. After that, come in the back door, there, and help me."

"Got it," Scott acknowledged, giving him a thumbs-up. "But what are you gonna be doing in there?"

"I have to rescue the animals before the basement floods."

"What time is it?" Dan asked, "Think my watch got waterlogged or something?"

Mike was lying next to him, on top of the two sleeping bags they'd spread out on the floor. It made it a bit more comfortable and cut down on the cold emanating from the damp concrete.

Mike pressed the button on his TIMEX to illuminate the dial.

"Two AM, buddy. I'll buy you a good watch when all this is over."

"Very funny," Dan grumbled.

"Wasn't meant to be." Mike explained. "Seriously, Dan, it's been one big nightmare, but having you along has made it easier. A LOT easier." "I agree, Mike," Dan said. "It's always good to have your best friend around so you have someone to blame."

Mike was about to respond when they heard noises upstairs.

"Back?" Dan whispered.

"Yeah, sure, Dan. Elsie forgot her knitting."

Dan was about to respond to that when the door to the basement suddenly opened.

Jack had gone about the business of implementing Stephanie's plan immediately. There wasn't much to actually DO, but there were a few things that needed to be done precisely in the time allotted.

He was just unlocking the door when a car rolled up. He opened the door enough to identify the vehicle as Stephen Drewers's. He threw open the door and waited for him to come inside with the box.

"Boy, I'm glad you still got it," Jack remarked. "It's going to make things a whole lot easier."

"Maybe," Stephen said cautiously. "Have you remembered how much of it went down the bowl?"

"No more than six or eight sheets," Jack answered.

"Ok, well, we should get away with it if no one decides to look for EVERY piece of paper that's supposed to be here." The both of them began to remove the files and sort them on the desk.

They didn't have much time left. The door leading out front, suddenly, opened, and Liz stuck her head in.

"We got a call," she informed them, with an ominous tone, "and you better take it."

CHAPTER 27

OPERATION BOOMERANG

Jerry left the driver's seat to see what was going on. He figured Elsie was involved because she was an integral part of every brawl so far. She wouldn't miss one unless she were unconscious or dead. He was paying so much attention to her, he almost stepped on Marge.

Marlene and Cheryl were laughing hysterically and forgot about Marge. Warren made his way forward to help Elsie, unaware that his spouse was in the middle of the chaos.

Elsie allowed him to pull her to her feet, and then she turned to face him.

"This is for what your wife did to me!" She spat, kicking him in the shin.

"OW!" Warren yelled.

Elsie looked at Marlene's horrified face and smiled.

"Anyone down there?" Virgil called. "Name is Parks. Jake sent me. Said someone might be stuck down there."

Silence. Mike and Dan were unsure of what to do next.

"Anybody there?" Virgil asked again.

"Parks?" Mike replied, finally. "You pulled us out of the mud yesterday, right?"

"Yep, that's me," Virgil replied. "Are you down there by yourself?"

Mike and Dan moved to the bottom of the stairs. "Just me and the Sgt. here," Mike answered.

They both took the stairs, but when they got to the top, Virgil made no attempt to move out of the way. Mike glared at Virgil and noticed a younger version of him standing behind him. Scott did look like his dad, with blue eyes, brown hair, and a rather big nose.

"Can we get through?" Mike asked, wondering why the man wouldn't move.

"We have to get going."

"Where to?" Scott asked, "It's pretty nasty out there." "Did they go down the mountain?" Dan asked.

"Who?" Virgil asked with a straight face.

"Whadd'ya mean, who?" Travers snapped, trying to get by. "Warner. Who else?" Travers made an attempt to get by, and Virgil raised his hand.

"Whoa, there, what's your hurry? It's pretty ugly out there, like my son just said. You also are gonna need a vehicle."

"There's one out there," Travers told him, taking a step forward.

The sudden move forced Virgil to take a step back, and Travers squeezed by along with Dan. All four wound up in the kitchen.

"I don't see a cruiser out there," Virgil observed, "if that's where you left it."

"You got here, didn't you?" Mike countered.

"Oh, now wait one minute, there, mister," Virgil said, pointing a finger at Mike's chest. "You ain't takin my truck, if that's what you're thinkin'."

"Our cruiser is stuck down the road," Dan said. "We haven't got a whole lot of time."

"Well, I'll be happy to pull it out for you, but you aren't taking my truck."

Mike and Virgil continued to glare at each other. "Why are you in such a hurry?" Scott asked.

"We're trying to catch someone," Dan explained, softly, as if he didn't want to be heard.

"Warner, right?" Virgil said with a smile. "Guess he got the jump on you, didn't he? Locks you up and takes off. Now, that's funny."

Mike's face turned red, but not out of embarrassment.

"Tell us where you're stuck," Scott offered, "and we'll pull you out in no time."

Dan tapped his furious friend on the shoulder.

"Come on, Mike," he said, "This guy needs his truck. Let's just do what he says and get going."

Mike, finally, grunted, which in his language meant he reluctantly agreed.

"Who's on the phone?" Jack asked as all three filed back into the radio room.

Jack couldn't help but notice that Liz was actually waddling.

"Trevor Doyle," Liz answered. "Sounds like he's got something planned, too."

Jack took the phone from Liz and shot a confused look at Drewer.

"Hello?" Jack answered, pulling a pen from his pocket and motioning to Liz for something to write on. He listened for a minute, then leaned over and wrote a message to his friends:

HE'S COMING DOWN HERE. NOW.

Elsie wasn't smiling very long.

Warren had hopped back a bit, then toppled over into the laps of Mike and Sharon. Jerry pulled Marge off the floor, just as Cheryl and Marlene went for Elsie.

The only person not involved in the melee did the only thing they could think of at the moment.

They slid into the driver's seat, dropped the van into gear, and stomped on the gas. The action immediately sent everyone hurtling backwards.

PIG PILE.

Virgil pulled his truck up as close as he dared to get a look at where the cruiser was stuck.

"Well," he pronounced, "I guess you ARE pretty stuck."

"Just pull us out and dispense with the smart remarks," Travers snapped.

Virgil put the truck in park, leaned across Dan, who was in the middle, and pointed a finger at Mike. Dan took a deep breath, hoping he wouldn't wind up in the middle if these two came to blows.

"Look here, Lieutenant," he warned, "I got a call in the middle of the night, which I could have easily ignored. My son and I came up here, in this nasty weather, just to let you loose. If you want my help, then start acting a little grateful, or I'll leave you both here and go home." "Are you sure this truck can get us out of that puddle?" Dan asked, trying to diffuse the situation.

"Yep. This truck may not look like much," Virgil said with pride, "but it's what's under the hood that counts."

Virgil put the truck in gear and began moving it into position, while Mike sat and seemed to sulk at being yelled at.

Jake took the news van screaming around the corner and through a stop sign, barely missing a light pole. The van seemed to balance on two wheels for a bit before settling back down on all four with a violent "thud."

It wasn't easy to ignore all the cussing and screaming going on behind him, but he was worried about getting them to Jericho by 4 am. The weather was rotten, but it and being the middle of the night pretty much guaranteed there'd be little traffic along the way. He blew through Underhill Center and its one blinking light, doing 60 mph.

He cringed when something crashed in the back and lit his pipe to calm his nerves.

"Can we find out where they are right now?"

Liz was chomping loudly on a carrot stick.

"Can we contact them somehow?"

"Not that I know of," Jack answered, sipping the sludge the station called coffee. "All I know is the time is set for four am. I'm sure they'll call if there's a problem."

"The weather is all they have to worry about, I guess," Liz observed.

The weather was only half the problem. The other was Jake's driving.

"Whoa, Nellie!" He yelled, taking another curve a bit too fast.

Something in the back came crashing to the floor, and a scream followed it. Stephanie climbed over Marge, Elsie, Warren, and Marlene to get to Jerry.

She held out her hand, which contained her cell phone. He reached for it and did so carefully, as if they were passing a bottle of nitroglycerin.

*STAR, TWO, SEVEN!" Stephanie yelled over the noise.

Jerry nodded as Stephanie seemed to disappear into the fray again.

Jake passed the community park doing sixty-five, and he knew he'd better slow down coming into Jericho. There were two ways to get to their destination, and Jake chose the back way rather than right down Main Street. He pumped the brakes, and that's when he discovered they were wet and not working well at all. The first turn was coming up soon, and he was going much too fast.

Liz was checking the stats on the latest NASCAR race when the phone rang. She was surprised to find it was her cell that was ringing, and even more so when she saw Stephanie's name on the caller ID.

"Stephanie?" she answered, "Where are you guys?"

There was a crashing sound, then a male voice came on and said two things.

The first made no sense at all, and the second caused her to panic.

"Jake! Slow down!!" Jerry yelled, "You're gonna get us killed!!"

Jake had a flashback to when he taught Elsie to drive. Her problem was remembering which pedal was which. His problem was one pedal wasn't responding very well.

"JAKE!" Jerry yelled, even louder, as he frantically fought his way to the passenger seat. He had to get past MARJE, who was lying on the floor with her feet up in the air. Jerry would think back on it later and wonder how she had gotten into that position in the first place. It was hilarious.

Jake pumped the brakes, but they showed little response. He took his pipe and stuffed it into his pocket. He saw the first turn coming, and it unnerved him.

"Oh Lord," he said, "this is gonna be hairy..."

Jack came running for the radio room and almost ran into Liz coming out. "JEEEZ, Lizzie," he said, coming to a stop just inches from her big belly.

"What the hell are you screaming about?" "BOOMERANG!" she replied, "and something's going on, 'cause someone's yelling something about someone getting everybody killed!" Jack's mouth dropped open, just enough to signify he was completely confused. He understood what "BOOMERANG" meant. Stephanie had chosen that as the code word for this crazy mission. She thought it fit well, considering everyone had left and was, now, coming back. "What?" Jack finally asked. "Tell me, but slowly."

Liz repeated herself, and Jack raised A HAND to silence her.

"They're on their way, but when?" Liz shrugged her shoulders.

"Let's assume their arrival is imminent," Jack said. "We need to..."

"Want some help?" came an unfamiliar voice.

Jack and Liz turned to see Trevor and Megan coming around the corner. Trevor was moving rather slowly but didn't appear to be in any pain.

"Yeah, they're on the way," Jack answered, relieved they had help. "Now what?"

"That's easy," Trevor replied. "We go open the door."

It hadn't taken much time to pull the cruiser out of its muddy grave.

Traver actually slipped Virgil $100 for helping them out. They rode down the mountain in silence, and just when they reached the bottom, Traver reached for the radio mike.

"Dispatch, this is Unit Seven, over," he began. "We have been out of touch for several hours and need updated information, over."

"Which way, Mike?" Dan asked, upon reaching the stop sign, "Jericho?" Mike answered, "I'm positive they went that way." They would need to gas up if they were headed anywhere else, and that's the closest."

The rain had let up a bit, but it was a short reprieve, as now it began to pour hard again. Dan turned up the wipers and made the left turn.

"Where do you think they're headed?" Dan asked. "I can't imagine where they'd hide now, do you?"

Mike gave up on the radio and hung up the mike. He lit a cigarette and stared straight ahead for a moment, giving it some thought. He didn't answer because he, really, had no idea.

Four mailboxes, 3 large shrubs, and a 20-foot length of white fence. That's what a news van can take down safely without flipping over on its side. Jake was still pumping the brakes and doing around 45 mph.

It was no longer a "pig pile" in the back, as everyone had been thrown to one side, along with a laundry list of items not tied down. The cussing and threats had given way to grunting and moaning, as everyone tried to comprehend what had just happened.

Jerry clambered over a duffel bag that had fallen from a shelf and made his way into the passenger seat.

"Jake," he started.

"Sorry about that," Jake interrupted, "the darn brakes are wet. Getting better, but it's still gonna be a rough ride, so tell 'em all to hang on."

"Jake, listen to me," Jake pleaded, "We can't take another corner like that."

Jake pulled his pipe and tobacco pouch from his pocket and shoved it in Jerry's face.

"Fill that up," he ordered, "an' let me handle this."

"But..."

"But, nothin'!" Jake shouted. "These brakes WILL dry out, but we have a couple more turns, so go back there and warn them!"

Jerry sat there, open-mouthed.

"After you fill my pipe, though," Jake added, then "UH OH. Forget the pipe."

"Are you sure about this?" Liz asked, looking at Trevor. "You realize we can get in a lot of trouble for this, right?"

"Liz," Jack coaxed, "we're gonna be in even more trouble if we don't do this."

"He's right," Trevor added, "We need to buy time, and this will get us the time we need."

"Yeah, but isn't this a bit much?" she asked. "You think they'll believe it and go for it?"
"Do you have a better idea?" Megan piped up.

Liz knew she was outnumbered. She leaned back in her chair, stretched, and then, after rubbing her big belly, she reached for the radio mike. Time to answer the call that had come in.

"Unit seven, this is dispatch, over."

The delayed response to their call startled them both. Mike jumped on the radio.

"Dispatch, this is unit seven, go ahead," he responded, eagerly.

"Unit one, what's your location, over?"

Mike took a quick look around and radioed back the information.

"Unit seven, hold your current position," the female voice ordered. "We are sending another unit to meet you."

Mike swore so vehemently that Dan jumped.

"Wait?" he nearly yelled into the mike. "What for? We are currently pursuing a vehicle and have no time to wait for an additional unit. We are continuing our pursuit."

Dan couldn't help wondering how you could pursue someone when you didn't know what direction they were headed in. He rolled his eyes, so Mike didn't see that or the smile that crept across his face.

Dan drove on.

"Perfect," Jack complimented, "Good job, Liz."

"Hold on, Jack," she disagreed. "How can it be perfect if they disobeyed the order?"

Jack examined his watch, then at Trevor, who was watching the clock on the wall. Liz and Megan looked at each other, realizing they had missed something.

Two more minutes passed, and Jack reached over to pick up the mike.

"Unit seven," he called, "please stop by the station for updated information on the subjects you are pursuing, over."

"Acknowledged," came the voice on the other end.

Jack looked at Liz and smiled.

"NOW, that's ABSOLUTELY PERFECT."

Jerry didn't have the time to warn anyone of the upcoming turn, and this time, Jake made it a wide one, taking down a mailbox and a stockade fence. He ignored the yelling and cuss words coming from behind him, choosing to light his pipe and pump the brakes some more. The third and last turn was coming up shortly, but the brakes seemed to be dry enough to make it an easy one.

"Jake," Stephanie called out to him from near the back of the van, "we need to park it out back, like last time, OK?"

"I figured as much, Jake mumbled to himself, giving her the thumbs-up."

"Jerry, how's everyone doin'?"

Jerry had gone to pull a couple of people off the floor and was just returning to the passenger seat.

"A little banged up," he answered, out of breath, "but it's a tough bunch; they'll live."

"Hope so," Jake said. "Remember, when this is over, they're still my neighbors..."

"You have my sympathies, my friend."

"Better warn them," Jake said sternly. "Last turn, one mile, and then one more to the station."

"Thanks, Jake," Jerry said, getting up and patting him on the shoulder.

"Don't thank me yet." Jake warned him. "Not yet."

Seventeen miles and twenty minutes was all that separated Travers and the van full of "escapees." Neither knew how close they were to one another. It would've been a completely different story if they did.

Dan and Mike had chosen to go right through Jericho by way of Main Street. They'd barely gone a mile when they came upon a downed wire, clear across the road. Dan turned the cruiser around.

"I'll take Belknap and come up the other side of it," he said.

"Power's out all through here," Mike observed. "It being Jericho, it should take days before it's back up."

There were several branches down on Belknap, but they were not so big that they had to stop and move them. They drove around them, and a couple minutes later,

They were back on Main. "Step on it, Dan," Mike said, flatly. "If you can, step on it."

CHAPTER 28

THE BOOMERANG EFFECT

The third turn was barely noticeable, considering the previous, hair-raising ones. Jake let out a deep sigh and relit his pipe.

Jerry passed the word that once they arrived, they needed to move fast.

Elsie and Mariene sat opposite each other, their eyes shooting daggers at the other. They had called a "time-out," ceasing hostilities for now, but they continued to lob insults and threats at each other, like two little girls on the playground.

"This ain't over." Elsie hissed.

"Darn right, it ain't," Marlene shot back. "You better hope we're not in the same cell, because I'll wipe the floor with that face of yours."

"I'd like to see you try," Elsie answered, with a sneer.

"Less than a mile, everyone!" Jerry yelled, "Get ready to move!"

"Are we all ready?" Trevor asked, looking from Liz to Jack to Drewer. Nods from all acknowledged they were ready to do their part.

"OK," Trevor announced, "Megan and I need to go. We shouldn't be here when everyone else gets here. You call me when it appears to be over. OK?" Nods from all, again.

Trevor shook hands with all, and then he and Megan left.

The news van came to a screeching halt by the back door. Jack had the door open and waved for them to come inside. Everyone on the van disembarked in less than two minutes, filing in to stand in the area between the holding cells.

"Everyone, listen up!" Jack yelled over the chatter. "This was Stephanie's idea, so she's gonna give you your instructions."

Stephanie grabbed a chair to stand on. She wanted to be able to see everyone's faces. She spent barely two minutes filling them in on what they had to do, and she noted that there were several smiles when they realized what was about to happen.

"Any questions?" she asked when she had finished.

Jake's hand went up.

"Yes, Jake?"

"I have to tell you," he said with a big grin, "you are a genius." A real genius."

One word from Jack and they all scattered.

Jerry started the van and waited for Cheryl, who had gone to the back to secure the doors. She finally made her way to the front and plopped down, hard, into the passenger seat. "I just had that 'déjà vu' feeling," she commented, removing her shoes to rub her tired feet.

"Me, too," Jerry said. "Last time it was a pickup, this time..."

"A BOOMERANG," Cheryl cut in.

"Sorry you didn't get the story you wanted so badly," he offered.

"Don't be," she replied. "I got my story. It's not the one I planned on, but I think it's even better." "OK, if you say so." Jerry conceded. "Buckle up, this might be a rough ride."

"Rough?" she asked incredulously. "Rough" is when Jake's driving. This will be a joyride compared to that."

They both were laughing as they left the parking lot and headed out of Jericho.

Dan pulled the cruiser up to the front door and had barely come to a stop when Mike opened the door to get out.

"This ought to be interesting," Dan observed as they made their way inside.

"They better have some good information," Mike warned. "I don't like wasting my time."

Both of them headed straight for the radio room, where they found Liz reading a James Patterson novel and drinking tea. She set the book down and leaned forward to put her elbows on the desk.

"Where have you guys been?" she asked. "We've been trying to reach you for hours and hours."

"We couldn't raise you, either," Travers replied. "What's this info you have for us?"

"Have you been up on the mountain since yesterday?" Liz queried, "What for?"

Mike looked to Dan, rolled his eyes, and then cleared his throat.

"Have you been sleeping through the last few days, or what?" He asked sarcastically. "We went up the mountain after that bunch of nuts from Knicker's Notch."

Liz eyed him for a few seconds. She wanted to irritate her boss but didn't want to get screamed at while doing it.

"Why? What was up there?" Mike's face grew to a crimson color, which made Liz sit back in her chair and roll it backwards a foot or so.

"What do you mean, what was up there?" Mike yelled. "They were! They tied me up and broke out of here, then we went up the mountain after them!!"

Liz picked up the phone. "Hey, yeah, can you come up here a minute? We've got a problem."

"Problem?" Mike shouted, "The only problem is you!"

A moment later, Jack wandered in, a coffee mug in hand. He was trying to appear calm and relaxed.

"Jack!" Mike yelled, "I put you on suspension!" You are NOT supposed to be here!"

"Yeah, well, when you took off on some wild goose chase, we were left short-handed," Jack explained. "They needed all the help they could get."

Mike was furious. Jack looked at Liz, which was her "cue" to speak.

"Lieutenant," she said, rather softly, "just WHO were you chasing?"

"Yeah," Jack added, "what people are you talking about? You're not making any sense..."

Dan stepped forward, seeing that Mike was very close to having his head blow off with rage.

Jack looked at Liz and smiled.

"What's so funny?" Mike demanded.

"Sergeant," Jack said, turning to Dan. "Would you follow me for a minute? There's something I'd like to show you."

Dan nodded, hoping whatever it was might serve to clear things up.

He followed Jack out of the radio room, leaving Liz with Travers, whose face had not changed in color.

"What's going on?" he asked her, trying to keep the anger out of his voice.

"Well, sir," she replied, cautiously, "I'm not sure you're alright." Did you have an accident or get drugged or something?"

Mike held back the urge to start screaming. This woman was pregnant, and that would be a good idea. He took a deep breath, exhaled slowly, and then answered her.

"Officer Palmer," he began slowly, "what are you insinuating?"

Liz was about to answer when Dan reappeared in the doorway, a look of shock and disbelief on his face. Mike hadn't seen that look very often through the years, but he knew something wasn't right.

"Dan? What's wrong?"

Dan opened his mouth, but it emitted no sound. He closed his mouth, closed his eyes for a few seconds, then reopened them, as if he thought the scene would change.

He held up a hand and gestured to Mike.

"I'll show you," he offered. "Come see this for yourself."

Stephanie's idea had been simple enough.

Return to the scene of the crime, and make it appear as if it never happened in the first place.

Everyone was in their original cell, wearing the same clothing. They'd pulled the McDonald's wrappers, cups, and bags from the trash and dispersed them throughout the cells. This made them appear inhabited for a while.

The evidence was piled on the desk, and Stephen Drewer sat there, reviewing it.

The bottom line was, if Trevor was not going to press charges against Elsie, then she should be released. The rest of the gang would be released because Judge Willis wouldn't allow Travers to try and charge them with anything. He couldn't charge them with escaping if he were unable to prove they left the jail in the first place. There was no evidence, and nobody was talking.

Dan had realized, instantly, what was going on and decided to go along with the plan. Doing so would mean this nightmare was finally over.

And it was.